Dare to Imagine

Dare to Imagine

Sydney vom Lehn

FORWARD MOVEMENT PUBLICATIONS
CINCINNATI, OHIO

Illustrations by Melissa Kelley

Cover Design by Robert Grove

© 2000
Forward Movement Publications
412 Sycamore Street, Cincinnati, Ohio 45202

CONTENTS

CHAPTER ONE
Emergency! 7

CHAPTER TWO
Unexpected Developments 16

CHAPTER THREE
Sunday Morning 36

CHAPTER FOUR
Storms and Anxiety 56

CHAPTER FIVE
Fame and Misfortunes 69

CHAPTER SIX
The Rescue 96

CHAPTER SEVEN
Daring to Imagine 112

CHAPTER ONE

Emergency!

Gina's father, David, swept through the kitchen gathering two sets of test papers, his grade book and a battered textbook. Gina knew right away why he looked upset. He had been up for hours getting the final proofs of his book ready to return to the publishers. Now he was late for the last faculty meeting of the year.

"Thanks," he said when she handed him a cold glass of orange juice. "I've got so much to do to get my grades in, I'll be late tonight." He drank the juice in two great gulps. "I forgot to tell Julia. Don't wait for me for dinner."

He walked around the table to where Gina's little sister was sitting. She looked pale and tired, not herself. David touched Beth's cheek gently and said, "When my school is over, honey, we'll have some fun."

In a moment he was gone. Gina's mother Julia came in. She poured herself a cup of coffee, put a piece of toast in the toaster.

"David said he'll be late tonight," Gina said.

"I'll be late too," Julia said. "I've got to finish typing my thesis. It's due tomorrow. There are some chicken pies in the freezer. Fix them and a salad for you and Beth and don't worry about us, okay?" Julia ate the toast without butter, drank the black coffee.

She looked at Beth. "You're not eating any cereal?"

"I'm not hungry," Beth said in such a quiet voice that Gina could hardly hear her. With her big brown eyes and delicate build, six-year-old Beth made Gina feel big and gawky.

Julia rinsed a few dishes in the sink.

"Well," she said, "I have to go. Take care of each other."

They heard the front door close. It was suddenly silent in the kitchen. Beth put her head down on the table. Gina came at once and sat down beside her.

"Tell me what's wrong, Beth."

"I don't feel good, that's all."

A stab of fear went through Gina. She put her hand on her sister's shoulder. "Why don't you go back to bed while I clean up the kitchen? I could read to you, then."

"Okay," Beth said with a sigh. She got up and

dragged herself out of the kitchen.

Gina put the coffee grounds down the disposal, put the orange juice back in the refrigerator. She had been looking forward to today, the first day of summer vacation. She was going to spend the whole summer writing stories. More than anything else she loved to write stories. Now she was really worried about Beth. Somehow she knew something was very wrong. When she went upstairs, she found Beth sound asleep.

She decided to work on her newest story about the adventures of a beautiful princess. Try as she would she just couldn't get into it. She knew Beth had a cold all last week. Beth didn't have colds very often and this one lasted so long. She walked back to Beth's room. Beth was lying flat in her bed. Her eyes were wide open. She was staring blankly at the ceiling. Tears were sliding down her cheeks.

"Beth! What is it?"

"Something terrible is happening to me," Beth wailed. "My head hurts, my throat hurts. Now it feels like pins and needles in my feet and hands. My knees are aching and so is my back."

Her teeth began to chatter with a strange little clicking sound.

"Hold on, Beth," Gina said. "I'll get David."

She rushed to the phone. The secretary's voice was cool and pleasant. Gina could hardly speak. She was breathless, close to hysterical.

"This is Gina Worthington," she blurted out.

"Tell my father Beth is terribly sick. Tell him it's an emergency. He must come home fast."

"Sure, Gina. Right away."

Gina dropped the phone and rushed back to Beth. She sat down on the bed and gathered her little sister in her arms. She rocked her back and forth and fear bonded the two of them.

She could hear David running fast, his feet pounding hard. He crashed through the front door, bounded up the stairs.

"What's wrong?" he shouted as he came.

"Beth is really hurting. Her head, her throat, pins and needles in her feet and hands, she aches all over."

"Let's get her to the infirmary."

Beth struggled to get out of bed. David caught her just as she started to fall. He looked grim. A muscle jumped near his jaw.

"Open the garage door, Gina." He wrenched the blanket off the bed and wrapped it around Beth.

He put Beth on the back seat of the car and Gina slid in beside her trying to comfort her. The engine roared. David drove swiftly to the infirmary.

A nurse instantly saw their panic and found the doctor.

"David," he said, "What's this?"

"Something is awfully wrong with Beth. She's hurting all over. Feels like pins and needles, she says. She can't stand up."

"Ah. Let's have a look."

The doctor bent over Beth. A nurse took her pulse. Another one put a blood pressure sleeve on her arm. The doctor listened to her chest with his stethoscope. Beth looked tiny and fragile on the big examining table.

"Pins and needles?" he asked. Beth made a strangled little sound. "Sore all over?" Beth just closed her eyes.

"I think I know what this is. I heard a lecture just lately about what they call Guillain-Barre Syndrome, GBS. It sounded so bizarre that I did some research on it. Then there was a long article in a medical journal about it. It's a paralyzing disease that strikes swiftly and then recedes slowly. I learned a doctor had better act fast, take no chances. Nurse, call an ambulance. Call the highway patrol, too. We may have to exceed some speed limits."

He turned to David.

"My friend," he said, "there are people at York University Medical Center just over the state line in North Carolina who can deal with this sort of thing. It's way beyond us here. She may need a respirator. We need to get her there fast."

Wrapped in her own peach-colored blanket, Beth was lifted onto a stretcher and carried out to the wide open doors of the waiting ambulance.

"I'll ride with her," the doctor said. "It's important that you and Gina be with her when we get there. It's a fact that ninety percent of people of every age who get this thing recover completely. But . . . it's going to be terrifying for her."

"For me, too," David said. "We'll be there."

The revolving red lights on the ambulance began to flash, but they didn't run the siren. They cleared cars and trucks out of their way as they went. They were out of Hansford and onto the highway in minutes. There, a silver and black highway patrol car was waiting. It roared ahead of them, flashing bright blue lights, and set the pace at over sixty miles an hour.

David drove intently. His hands gripped the steering wheel. His body leaned forward. He followed the ambulance closely.

"I'm really scared." Gina had to say it.

"We're both scared, Gina. I have this awful feeling we are confronting stark evil here. It's bigger than we are; we can't control it. It's hitting someone we love."

Suddenly a siren made a piercing shriek. The ambulance zipped by the patrol car, took off at breakneck speed. David sped up and as they passed the patrol car, Gina could see the officer talking into his car phone. As they cruised by him, he put on his screaming siren too. The three vehicles shot along the highway, hurtled onto an off ramp, blazed down a wide avenue.

The area around the hospital was quite used to sirens day and night, but this arrival made people turn around and look. Gina couldn't control the trembling that shook her whole body.

"Oh God!" David said fervently.

The ambulance pulled up at the emergency entrance and before anyone could get out, there were efficient people all around, ready to take care of Beth.

David ran to her. Gina saw one of the attendants take hold of both David's arms. He spoke to him urgently. David stood back, watching as they rushed Beth into the hospital.

One time Gina had slipped on some ice and hit her head on the sidewalk. It knocked her breath out. The shock of the blow stunned her. This felt the same way.

David came back, parked the car in a visitor space. "I got told to wait in the emergency waiting room," he said. They walked together into the hospital. No one was there. They found the waiting room and sat down uncomfortably. Almost at once a young intern arrived.

"They've taken your daughter to the intensive care unit on the top floor, Dr. Worthington. She's under severe stress."

"Do you know what happened on the road?"

"I understand she started choking, which is alarming in these cases. It's been controlled now, but she may require a respirator at any moment. This thing attacks the breathing system. What we take for granted, what ordinarily works automatically, gets attacked. It's weird."

"What now?"

"They'll want you and Gina up there as soon as they get her settled in. She needs both of you desperately."

The elevator took them up like a rocket. The doors opened on a vast semicircle of blue carpet with five double doors. The intern led them through the central one, around another circular hallway and then into a small waiting room.

"I know this is tough," the intern said to Gina. "I hear it was your call and you made the right one. You probably saved her life. Now let us do what we can."

He left them, promising to keep in touch. The only sound was the click of the wall clock as it went from minute to minute.

"I hope Julia is okay," Gina said.

"Julia," David said, "has always been the strength of this family. Whenever I need her most, she's there. She puts up with my crazy notions, my crazy dreams, my . . . theology. She's practical, I'm not. She's patient, I'm not. And besides all that she's beautiful. I love her so much."

"I know she loves you just as much," Gina said, "only I wish she was here."

"My office and the infirmary both will call her. There was no time to lose, you know. She'll understand that. I hope she brings us our tooth brushes."

The doctor came in.

"For now, they've decided not to put her on a

respirator. They're doing extensive tests, MRI and catscans, and, unfortunately, a spinal tap. Poor Beth! But there's a fellow with her who's a genius with kids. He actually got Beth to smile. There's a message from your wife. She'll be here any minute."

"Thanks for all you've done, Doctor," David said sincerely.

"You're in good hands now. I'll be praying for all of you."

CHAPTER TWO
Unexpected Developments

The family was plunged into a whole new world. The routine of the hospital became their routine. Day after day seemed to be the same, yet day after day new things happened to Beth. She could not move at all. Somehow they got used to that. At first there were several tubes attached to her. Then a pleasant therapist started gently moving her arms and legs. He curled and uncurled her fingers, turned her head from side to side. Every morning she had to blow as hard as she could into a strange instrument. Then they hooked her onto a plasmapheresis machine which cleans and replaces blood so that the body makes the kind of cells necessary to heal damaged nerves. They were all worried about it the first time, but after the third treatment, Beth seemed to get much better. With all the attention she was getting, Beth seemed not quite so terrified. One morning Beth's favorite nurse, Mrs. Turner, was replacing a splint on her foot that prevented what they called "foot drop." Beth cried out. "Ouch!"

Mrs. Turner said, "Oh Beth! I know it seems awful to be glad something hurts, but it means you're getting better."

David had long talks with Jim Benedict, the hospital chaplain. Gina liked him; he made Beth laugh. Once in a while he would ask David to sit with a frightened patient.

"This is such a big place," he said, "we really need more than one minister. All the ministers of York churches visit a lot, but so many patients don't go to any church. They're usually the ones who need help the most."

So Beth gradually began the long road to recovery. So did Gina and Julia and David. Julia graduated, *magna cum laude,* in absentia. David kept getting calls from Eliot Brown who reported the news that David's book had been published and there was a great review in the New York Times by an important scholar. Then came the news that it was selling better than anyone expected.

Jim Benedict found them a faculty apartment that would not be occupied until fall semester. It was in the center of the beautiful campus. It delighted Gina. Looking out the window at the tall spires of York University Chapel seemed to her to be looking out on the imaginary land of kings and queens, princes and princesses that she loved. She could hear the magnificent carillon in the bell tower. She found, in the York Gardens, a place of peace and beauty.

Unfortunately there were bills, big bills. Much of Beth's treatment wasn't covered by David's health insurance. Again, the chaplain helped. He arranged for David to teach two summer school classes and tutor several graduate students in Greek. He found a job for Julia as an assistant to Professor Glover in the Art Department. So they had a place to stay until fall and some income, which was essential.

David said, "We need your help, Gina. Julia and I can work only if you can take care of Beth. Mrs. Turner will be here every morning. I'll get home for lunch. They'll send a physical therapist every afternoon. But Beth needs someone with her all the time, every minute."

On the first Sunday of August they brought her home to their apartment. It was a joyful day but Gina kept thinking, how can I keep her happy? Then it came into her mind as clear as crystal: she would share her princess story, day by day, making it last for a long time, and they could read as many books as she could find in the York library about castles in England and stories about people who lived in them. There would be acres of books like that in the York library. So instead of dreading Monday morning when David and Julia would have to go to work, she looked forward to it eagerly. Julia and David hugged her, then hurried away together.

Right away she said to Beth, "How would it be if I told you about the story I'm writing about a beautiful princess?"

"You could tell it to me?"

"I thought it would be fun for both of us. Look at this picture of a castle with deep, dark water all around it. See the turrets and towers and high stone walls? The tallest round tower, this one, is where the princess lives."

"How old is the princess?" Beth wanted to know.

"She's fifteen, like me. Her name is Victoria. Her father is King Richard, a rich and powerful king. He owns all the land around the castle for hundreds of miles."

"Is the queen beautiful?" Beth asked eagerly, and Gina knew that her idea was going to work.

"Yes, Queen Anne is beautiful, but she is sad. The princess is her only child, and she's a girl. The king needs a son so he can be sure there is someone young to rule his kingdom when he gets old. But it was not to be."

"Victoria could rule the kingdom, couldn't she?"

"Not in those days. The reason there were castles to begin with was because there was always someone who wanted to take your kingdom

19

away from you, someone stronger or with a bigger army, or with new weapons that smashed the castle walls."

"Tell me more about Victoria."

"Everyone loves her. She's always happy, full of sparkling life. She has long, golden hair like yours, and sometimes they put a circlet of pearls like a crown on her head. She has lovely royal costumes, but she would rather dress in homespun like her friends. They are the children of the castlefolk. One of them is Justin. He's a bit older than Victoria, and already he can swim, ride like the wind, and handle a sword like an expert. Because his mother has been her nurse ever since she was born, Justin is Victoria's special friend."

Downstairs someone was knocking on the door.

"That will be Mrs. Turner, Beth. I'll go let her in."

She ran downstairs.

"How's our patient today?" the white uniformed nurse said cheerfully, coming in with her black bag.

"She's been eating better. I think that's helping."

"I'm sure it is. And how are you doing?" She asked as if she really cared.

"Fine, thanks, now that Beth is better," Gina said, leading Mrs. Turner up to Beth's bedroom.

Just then the bell tower sang out. Gina stopped to listen. "Oh, I love the sound of those bells!" she said. "I don't know what it reminds me of, something mysterious inside me, calling to me." When the hour began to toll eleven, they walked on up the steps.

"Good morning, young lady," Mrs. Turner said with a big smile. "You look better every day." She went through the familiar routine, taking Beth's pulse, temperature and blood pressure. She listened to her heart with a stethoscope. Then she took Beth's hands in hers and asked her to squeeze as hard as she could.

"It hurts?" she said, kindly, as Beth winced.

"Really hurts," Beth said, "and I still feel crawly things under my skin."

"That will go away, I promise you," Mrs. Turner said. "But what got hurt has to mend. You've been so brave and patient with all this pain. We are proud of you. Believe me, Beth, I've seen many people, young and old, go through this and get on with their lives as if nothing happened. Would you like me to rub your back?"

Beth smiled. "Yes, thank you. You're the best back rubber."

They laughed, and Gina went to look out the window while Mrs. Turner tended to Beth.

She could see lots of students in shorts and sandals. Along the path to the chapel she could see carefully tended borders of bright summer flowers. They made her think about York Gardens. In those first, fearful days her mother and she would walk together in the gardens, trying to forget their constant fear that Beth was too sick to live.

"You're doing just fine, Beth. You are a good patient," Mrs. Turner said when she put all her instruments back in her bag. Then she turned to Gina. "I brought a copy of your father's book with me today. I hoped he might autograph it for my son. I want him to read it. I just love it!"

She put the book in Gina's hands. The title *Journey Into Light* and the drawing of a spectacular star on the cover still fascinated her. On the back was a picture of David looking young and joyful. How happy they had been on the day Eliot Brown called to say that *Journey Into Light* was going to be published. Two days later they took Beth to the hospital.

"Will you tell him it's for Kevin Turner? He's a counselor at a boys' camp in Maine this summer, teaching fencing and horseback riding."

"Kevin Turner, what a nice name. Sure, I won't forget."

"Beth is doing all right," Mrs. Turner said downstairs, just before she left. "But none of us knows how long this will take. A fine family like yours is the very best medicine. With love and faith she'll get well."

"Julia and David spend every minute they can with her. They play games with her, they read to her. They help her do all her exercises. David makes crossword puzzles for her."

"Julia? David?" Mrs. Turner looked puzzled. "Not Mom and Dad?"

Gina laughed. "My father calls my mother Julia. My mother calls him David. When I was little, they told me that's who they are. Even his students call him David at home in Hansford."

Mrs. Turner put a kind hand on Gina's arm. "Do you get homesick, Gina?"

"Sometimes. I miss my friends. I keep wondering what they are doing and who's going with who, now. But York is really beautiful. I love the chapel. I love the gardens."

"They are 'specially beautiful now that the roses are blooming. Monday when I come I'll stay long enough for you to go look at them."

"Thanks, Mrs. Turner, thanks."

She was surprised to find Beth sound asleep again when she went back upstairs. She sat down quietly in the rocker by the bed, closed her eyes and started thinking about what was going to happen to the pretty princess and her friend Justin.

She had a picture of him in her mind. He had dark, smiling eyes and a tiptilted nose. He wore brown woolen tights and a forest green tunic with a red belt. He wore a jaunty hat with a pheasant feather. He had black, curly hair. He looked strong and healthy and summer tanned . . . Justin.

She pictured him swimming in the water

around the castle, fencing skillfully with the other boys, riding bareback recklessly across wide fields with the wind blowing his hair. Leaning over the parapet outside the arched door into the tower where the princess lived, he would wait for her to come out and talk to him, knowing he was her favorite friend. He would look at the land that belonged to the king, fertile land with prosperous farms and flocks of sheep and forests of tall timber. This was Warwick, and one day it would belong to Victoria, as soon as she found a prince to marry her and defend her kingdom. And here was a fact that had to be faced, no matter how it hurt. Justin was not a prince; he was the son of one of the king's men, a soldier of many campaigns, known and trusted, but of common blood.

Gina tried to figure out what was going to happen in the story. Somehow it had to be possible for Justin, the hero, to marry the princess and live happily ever after. She thought about making him a prince after all, rescued as a child from a burning castle by the soldier he called father. But somehow, no matter what, Justin just refused to be changed into a prince.

Putting that difficulty aside for now, Gina started thinking about how the princess, in spite of all the things she had to do as a royal princess, liked to be an ordinary girl. Maybe Victoria would dress in a boy's clothes and bribe the stableman not to interfere, to let her ride with Justin on one of her father's finest horses. Justin would teach her to ride astride, racing across the fields, scattering the sheep.

Gina thought about York Gardens. Of course the castle gardens would be just like them. She pictured Victoria and Justin walking there together. In her imagining, she was Victoria, and Justin was her dear friend. Being with this wonderful, exciting, handsome person filled her with great joy.

"This is crazy," she told herself.

Beth didn't wake up until it was time to fix lunch.

"Go on with the story, Gina, please. Please, Gina, please?" Beth insisted. "I'm not hungry now. I want to hear the story."

"You will be hungry by the time I fix your favorite sandwich. Besides, I have to figure out what happens next."

In the kitchen she sliced a juicy tomato, shredded up some crisp lettuce and started to cook bacon in the frying pan. It was just beginning to curl up, when her father came in.

"Wow, Gina, that smells wonderful!" he said with a grin. "Got enough for me?"

"Sure," Gina said, fishing the strips out of the sizzling fat and draining them on a piece of paper

25

towel. Her father went upstairs to see Beth. Working quickly, she made sandwiches, poured some milk in a glass for Beth and added the vitamin supplement that turned it into a foamy chocolate milkshake. She measured out the coffee and water and turned on the coffee maker for her father. He came into the kitchen, rolling up the sleeves of his white shirt. Gina looked at him and thought maybe her handsome Justin looked a lot like her father. He caught her looking at him fondly and said, "What?"

"Just glad to see you, I guess. And oh! Mrs. Turner brought a copy of your book for you to autograph. She said she loved it. She's really nice, so could you write something special for her son? His name is Kevin Turner."

"I can do that," he said, getting out a coffee cup. "We'll take all this upstairs, okay? I hate to leave Beth alone."

"She's ever so much better, don't you think? It's not so scary any more."

"For me, I'll never be the same. If only I hadn't been so busy teaching all day, writing my book all night. I was self-concerned. I didn't notice what was happening."

"She did have a cold. She was pretty droopy. But until the GBS symptoms begin, there's no way of knowing a person is getting so sick. I heard them telling you that more than once."

"Julia feels bad, too, I know. It haunts her. She

blames herself for being busy, too, keeping up with her classes, writing her thesis. Maybe we could have gotten help sooner."

"Kids get colds all the time, even bad virus colds, and it's not GBS."

"Guilt, you see. One of the very things I write about in my book. I blame myself. I can't shake it. I can't help Julia shake it. I can't seem to forgive myself, or feel forgiven, even though I'm the one who is telling other people how to do that."

They took the lunch upstairs and Gina set out the little pink table they had found to put across Beth's lap for a lunch tray.

"The bacon smelled so good, Gina, it did make me hungry. You were right. But you've got to go on with the story."

"What story?" her father wanted to know.

"It's neat," Beth said, taking a big mouthful of sandwich. "About a princess and a boy who likes her."

David Worthington gave his older daughter a quizzical look.

"Scheherezade?" he said, lifting an eyebrow.

"What's that?" Beth asked.

"Well, she was an Arabian princess who fell into the hands of a wicked man who had a bad habit of killing off his wives. Scheherezade kept him from killing her by telling him stories. Every night she kept him in suspense about how the story ended."

"Sort of like they do on TV soap operas?"

"Exactly."

"Julia says no soap operas," Beth said with a sigh.

"Gina's stories are probably a whole lot better. She makes good sandwiches, too, doesn't she? Thanks, Gina."

After lunch, before he closed himself up in his study, David gave Beth a crossword puzzle he had made for her. It was a big one but she had it done in no time. She showed it to Gina proudly.

"Go tell David I did it!" she said.

"He's working, Beth. Let's not interrupt him."

"Then you have to go on about Victoria. What happened next?"

Gina got a rocking chair and pulled it up by the bed.

"Close your eyes and rest," she said.

"When you tell me a story, I forget about being sick. That's really resting."

"Okay, then, here's what happened. The king decided he was going to choose a husband for Victoria so that all the world would know that his kingdom had an heir who would defend it when he was old. He told Victoria that there were three princes who would come, one by one, and she could decide which one she would marry. But Victoria was not happy about it, and she told her father that she would never marry anyone who wasn't as strong, as smart and as handsome as Justin."

"Oh," Beth said, "no one could be as good as Justin."

"Well, so here the first one came."

"Was he nice?"

"I think so, yes."

"How did Justin feel about it?"

Gina stopped to think. How would he feel, having to take on these men in a competition he couldn't win? What reward could the king give him for proving these men?

"Maybe the king would let him marry Victoria if he was better than any of them," Beth declared.

Gina shook her head. "No. He couldn't do that. Justin doesn't have royal blood."

"That's silly," Beth protested. "All blood is the same. David said that. All humans have the same blood."

"This was a different time. People believed differently. They thought the world was flat. They didn't know we are a little planet among big planets and that we go around the sun, the sun doesn't go around us. There was a big difference between royal people and common people in those days."

Gina felt very sad for Justin.

"So go on, Gina!" Beth ordered.

"The first prince who came was Henry of Lancaster. Now Lancaster was just as big as

Warwick, and Henry's father was almost as rich as King Richard. He had two sons, Charles and Henry. Because Charles was the oldest he would inherit Lancaster. But if Henry could marry Victoria and inherit Warwick, the two brothers together would be incredibly powerful."

"But was he nice? Did Victoria like him?"

"The funny thing was that Justin liked him, liked him a lot. They were the same age, they liked the same things, like riding and archery and swimming. But the thing they really loved was fencing, and they were both so good at it that many soldiers would watch them and marvel at how well matched they were."

The story was beginning to fascinate Gina. She went on, "Victoria was angry, very angry. 'You spend all your time with this Henry; he spends all his time with you. What about me?' she shouted at Justin one day. Justin just smiled at her. He had never had a friend like Henry before, someone like a twin. His smile infuriated the princess. She went storming off to the king. She told him that since Justin liked Henry so much she would just choose him and be done with all the foolishness of other princes coming.

"'Victoria, you must give the others a chance,' the king declared. Victoria was very stubborn.

"'I've made up my mind. I'll see the others, but you must know that no matter what they're like, I'll choose Henry because Justin thinks he's so fine.'

"So the king called Henry in and told him what she had said. To his great surprise and dismay, Henry said, 'Sir, I have decided that I am not willing to take on this great responsibility. I am honored, but I feel absolutely sure that I must know more of the world in order to become a proper king. My father is going to tour the continent next month, and I want to go with him. We will visit the royalty in France and Germany and Italy. We will see their cathedrals, their castles and fabulous formal gardens. My mother wants to find an Italian landscaper to fashion a garden for Lancaster, to be the showplace of the whole country.'

"'Go your way, Henry. This matter can wait a while,' the king said, much taken with Henry's good looks and enthusiasm."

The story suddenly took an unexpected turn. Gina couldn't believe it, it just happened. She said, "Guess what happened?" almost to herself.

"What?" Beth was wide-eyed and breathless.

"Henry took Justin with him, back to Lancaster, and pursuaded him to go abroad with his family."

"No!"

"Yes! Justin had never been more than a few miles from the castle in his whole life and he was thrilled. So one day, just like that, Justin was gone."

"Poor Victoria!" Beth said. "How lonely for her."

"Well, she had those other friends, and the other

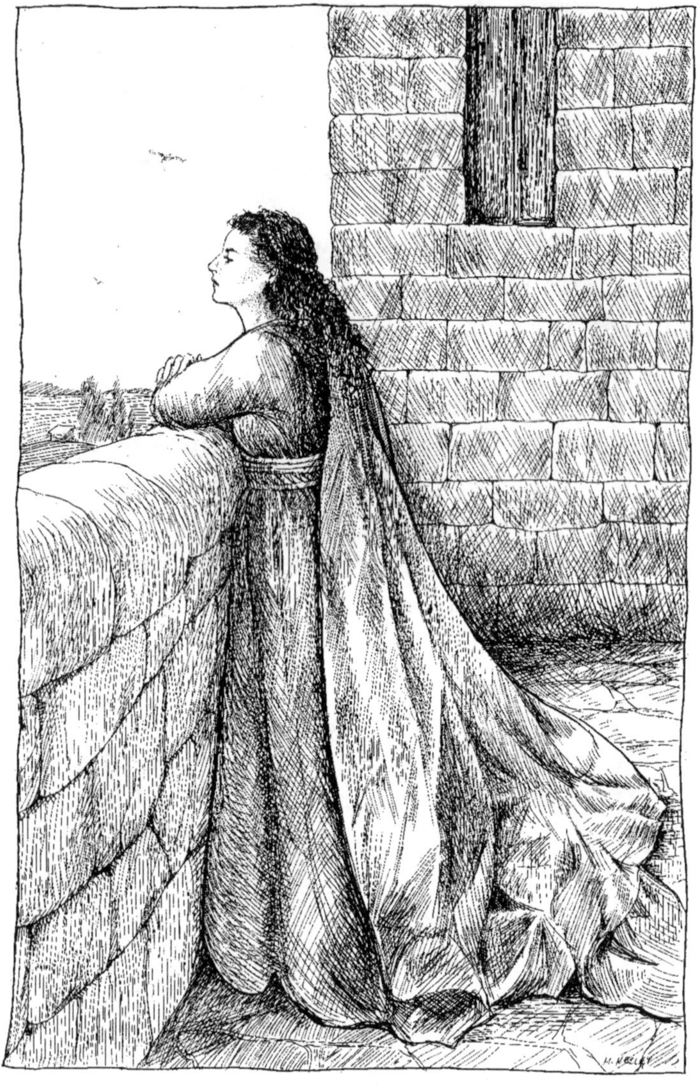

two princes were coming, but she missed Justin badly, and the fact that Henry had turned her down made her both sad and angry. When she was angry, she was not a very pleasant person."

The telephone rang downstairs. Gina hurried to answer it. Then she went and knocked on her father's study door. "Telephone for you, David. It's Eliot."

She heard him say, "Eliot! Good to hear from you."

She went to the kitchen and fixed another milkshake for Beth. It was a special kind of nutritious milkshake that she drank twice a day to regain the weight she had lost.

While she drank it, Gina looked out the window thinking hard about Victoria. Then she saw a familiar figure. It was Beth's physical therapist, Joanie. She looked like a young college student. In just a minute she was with them.

Gina helped her spread a mat on the floor. Together they helped Beth out of bed and down onto it. Then Gina left them while the exercise session began.

She was in the kitchen, reading, when Julia came home.

"How is everything?" she asked. "Did you have a good day? What did Mrs. Turner say?"

"Beth is doing fine," Gina said. "Joanie is with her now."

"I'm glad. These days are awfully long for me.

I keep wishing I could be with you both all day. I keep worrying about you."

They went upstairs to Beth's room. Joanie was lifting Beth back into bed.

"I've worn her out, I'm afraid. It has to be that way for a while. Then it will get easier. I have to be a little mean."

"You aren't mean, Joanie," Beth said, sounding tired. "I know you aren't mean."

Joanie laughed and leaned over to kiss Beth. "Good-bye, then, sweetheart, until tomorrow."

Just after she left, David came rushing into the room.

"Ah, you're home," he said, putting his arms around Julia. "Eliot called. Wonderful news! The book is on the best-seller list! Imagine! I can't believe it! Eliot is full of wild ideas again. Wants me to fly to New York on Friday to tape an interview for the Morning Show. Would you believe he wants to fly me up there, put me up, feed me and ferry me around, all for a four minute interview about the book?"

"What did you say?" Julia asked.

"I said I'd have to ask you first, Julia."

"Do you want to go?"

"Eliot has gone to so much trouble to set this up for me over a weekend so I won't have to cut any classes. I'd feel bad about refusing but . . ." He walked over to Beth's bed, looked down on her lovingly.

"New York!" Gina exclaimed. "The Morning Show! That's terrific!"

"You're impressed?" David turned to her with a smile.

"We're all impressed, David. You must go. We'll be fine." Julia hugged her husband.

"We'll watch the show," Beth said joyfully.

"I'll probably watch it with you, since it won't air until Monday morning. But what can I say in four minutes about a book that took me two years to write?"

"Eliot will tell you," Julia said, laughing.

And so, suddenly, David Worthington was gone. He hadn't been gone ten minutes before a feeling of worry came over Gina. David was central to her life. Because he was always close to her she felt protected, secure, safe. He had always been there for her.

It's only a few days, she told herself. Don't be childish. But the feeling wouldn't go away that somehow she was on her own, and whatever happened, she would have to handle it herself.

CHAPTER THREE
Sunday Morning

Gina and her mother spent the morning doing housework. They changed all the beds, did a big wash, cleaned the whole apartment and made a casserole that would last two days. Then Julia said, "It's time you do what you want to do."

"I'm fine," Gina said, but she thought to herself that if they were home in Hansford she'd go to the library or to the ice cream store and her friends would be there. Hansford, with its square brick college buildings, wasn't much to look at, but she belonged there. She knew everyone, and everyone knew her.

Her mother finished washing the dishes in the sink and wiped her hands on her apron.

"Why not have a walk in the gardens?" she said, "I hear the roses are spectacular."

"So Mrs. Turner said."

"It would do you good. You haven't been out of the house for days. It may get hot this afternoon, but it's lovely now."

Maybe it might help me make up more story, Gina thought. She remembered how she had imagined Victoria and Justin walking in the garden. She changed into a cool sleeveless blouse and her favorite shorts and sandals. She went to tell Beth where she was going but her sister was fast asleep again. She found her mother with test papers spread all over the kitchen table.

"This being an assistant to Professor Glover is getting to be a ton of work," she said. "If we didn't need the money for Beth's bills I wouldn't do it. At first all I did was listen to his fine lectures and take notes. Now he's got me correcting his quiz papers as well as typing up my notes to hand out to the class. He's a dear old man, and I want to keep him happy, but really!"

"How many tests?"

"Forty-five." Julia groaned. "It'll take me all afternoon."

"I'll be back in a little while," Gina said. "Maybe I could help you?"

"We already ask too much of you, honey," Julia said, hardly looking up from the paper in front of her. "Enjoy the gardens."

So she walked across the campus and down the road by the towering medical center building. She felt the sun, hot on her head. There wasn't a breath of wind to cool the air. She was glad when she reached the wooded path to the York Gardens. She walked in the shade and began to think about Victoria and Justin.

He would cross the English Channel in style with Henry and his father. Then they would ride in a procession of elegant carriages with fine horses and footmen and guards in the king's uniforms. A great banner with the Lancaster coat of arms would be carried proudly at the head of the procession. There would be the sound of wheels turning fast and swords clinking, and when they arrived at a castle, there would be trumpets calling.

Justin would be dressed in a velvet tunic now, with fine silk hose and splendid leather boots with silver buckles, and a great big hat with sweeping feathers. He and Henry, together, would be welcome wherever they went, healthy, high spirited and good looking. Henry's father was delighted with Justin, with his wit and good nature. He was thankful his son had found such a splendid companion.

But Victoria had lost her best friend. He wasn't there, leaning over the parapet, waiting for her. He wasn't there to ride with her, wasn't there to walk in the gardens with her. She spent all her time alone, refusing to be with her friends. She retreated into loneliness, pale and silent. Queen Anne was very worried about her.

Gina walked through the gates to the first view

of the gardens. Roses of every color bloomed on both sides of the path—vivid red and scarlet, pale pink and creamy white. Gina was delighted. The scent filled the air around her. She stopped, just letting the sight and the perfume surround her.

There were quite a few people there, walking and talking quietly. She saw many couples. She tried to imagine Justin there with her but she knew she was very much alone. Try as she might, she couldn't think of a way she could get Justin back into the story. He seemed to have disappeared completely, off with Henry, far away, gone. She could feel Victoria's loneliness inside her. She sat down on a cool bench.

I shouldn't have let that happen, Gina told herself. Why did I have to make such an awful problem for them? Then she remembered that they already had a problem because Justin wasn't a prince. She had tried to make him into one, but he just wouldn't be changed. He was the son of a soldier, devoted to the king.

Maybe the next prince would simply sweep Victoria off her feet, now that Justin was gone. Maybe, without Justin being there to compete against him, he would pay lots of attention to Victoria and make her happy.

Gina got up and started walking again. She came to a little lily pond that she loved. Beside it stood a statue of an angel with a lovely, serene face. At the hospital when Beth was so sick, she had asked her father about angels.

"They say," he told her, "that angels are messengers of God. People have been making images of them for ever so long. The idea of a guardian angel is that each of us is cared for in a very special way. An angel, then, is a way of thinking about God's love for each of us."

Gina remembered saying, "I'd like to think that Beth has a beautiful guardian angel."

And David said, "I look at the faces of some of her nurses, and I can see they love her. Maybe they are angels in disguise."

Now the loneliness swept through Gina. She missed her father, missed his smile, missed the sound of his voice, just missed him.

Then a cheerful voice said, "Gina! Hi!" It was Mrs. Turner. She seemed always to have a book in her hand. "Isn't this the most wonderful place? Did you know that all these beautiful formal gardens are designed like the gardens the monks kept inside the walls of their monasteries? They grew their vegetables and fruit trees and herbs. The flowers were for the altars of their churches. They even kept fish in a pond for Friday meals when they couldn't eat meat."

"I love gardens."

They sat down on a bench by the angel and looked at the book together. There were pictures of gardens in England, in France, in Italy.

"Look at this one," Mrs. Turner said, pointing

to a spectacular color plate. "This one is in Italy today. It has been there since the twelfth century. Look at the design, isn't it perfect?"

They fell silent, both studying the picture. Gina was imagining people in that garden . . . Justin.

"I'll be glad to lend you this book," Mrs. Turner stood up. "I'm so glad I found you here. See you on Monday."

When Gina got home her mother was helping Beth with her reading so Gina went to her own room. She sat on the bed and looked at the color plate more closely. She tried to smell the flowers, feel the cool water blowing from the fountains, be there, and think of Justin being there. It was no use. She felt lonely again.

The book Mrs. Turner wanted autographed was on her dresser. She got up and looked at the picture of her father on the jacket. It just made her ache even more. You're really feeling sorry for yourself, aren't you, she told herself. Better do something constructive. She went to the kitchen and started supper.

The three of them ate together, and then Julia went back to her work.

Beth said, "Tell me some more about the princess, Gina?"

"I can't," she answered. "I don't know what's happening."

"You've got to get Justin back."

"How can I do that?"

"Well, you're the one making it all happen, aren't you?"

"I thought I was," Gina said with a frown, "but somehow what happens isn't up to me any more."

Beth laughed. "I'll make it up, then!"

"What happens?"

Beth covered her face with her hands and sat very still. Then she said in a small voice, "I don't know."

"Maybe it will come to one of us overnight. Sometimes that happens, if I'm listening."

"Listening to what?" Beth asked.

"Just for ideas, I guess."

"I miss David." Beth's voice was full of sadness.

Gina tried to be cheerful. "He'll be back tomorrow night."

"I know . . ." Beth turned her head, hiding sudden tears.

Gina quickly got her mother to come and comfort Beth. Then she went to her room feeling more lonely than she had ever been in her life. She couldn't go to sleep for a long time. She blamed herself for making Beth sad, too. She kept trying to think of ways to make the story come out right. Nothing worked.

She decided she would try really hard to picture the inside of the castle. She wanted to imagine exactly what Victoria looked like and what she might be doing tonight.

Suddenly, there was the Great Hall of Warwick

Castle. It was noisy and crowded, with servants serving a huge meal to dozens of people seated on benches at wooden tables, drinking out of tankards, shouting and laughing hilariously. It was a feast like no other she had ever seen. She found herself carrying two huge baskets of fragrant fresh-baked bread. Sitting all together were many rough looking men. One of them reached out and took a big piece of bread from a basket.

Gina put down the baskets. Grabbing hands emptied them both in a minute.

"So he's come back," a large, beefy looking man said, loudly. "He may have been a pilgrim to the Holy Land, but you can be sure he's up to no good."

"Watch your tongue, Kensington, he's still the king's brother."

"Fetch some more brew, wench," Kensington barked at Gina. "The only good thing about him coming back is the celebration."

Gina had no idea where to go or if she could manage the enormous pitchers she saw sitting on the tables. She picked up an empty one and followed a man carrying two of them. If the Great Hall was noisy and crowded, the castle kitchen was far worse. People bumped into each other as they went about their duties, everything from pulling bread out of the great, hot oven to carving huge roasts onto platters that looked as round as wagon wheels.

"How many men has he with him?" she heard someone ask.

"At least a hundred, all hungry."

"So they'll stay here?"

"Not for long. Those two brothers never liked each other."

Gina slipped out of the kitchen, intent on seeing Victoria.

At a long table on a raised platform sat the royal family. The king and his brother, the queen and Victoria. Gina was thrilled with her. She looked every inch a princess. She remembered Beth asking if the queen was beautiful, and there she was, beautiful indeed. The king, a gold crown perched on his head, looked regal but nice, too. His brother, George, had a very thin face, a pointed nose and a trim black curly beard.

Gina watched Victoria, and somehow that made Victoria notice her. She beckoned to her. Gina went to her.

"Are you with Uncle George's company?" she asked.

Gina shook her head. "I've just come in from the country," she said. "They needed help in the kitchen."

"Indeed they do. This is the biggest banquet ever at Warwick. But I know I have seen you before. What's your name?"

"My name is Gina."

"Regina! That means queen, of course."

"I am not of royal blood."

"You appear to be, though. Have you a sister, perhaps, one who might have been here at the castle?"

"I have a sister, but she's much younger than I.

She's never been to this castle."

"Come," Victoria said, "Sit down here beside me. I want to talk to you."

She slid over and made room for Gina to sit down.

"This royal blood business makes me sick," Victoria sighed.

"What do you mean?"

"I have a friend . . ."

"Justin," Gina said before she thought.

"How did you know that?" Victoria demanded and her voice sounded harsh.

What would you say, Gina thought, if you knew that I'm the one who created him? Suddenly everything started to whirl around. A fight had broken out between some of George's men and the king's men. The fight got louder and louder with crashing tables and women screaming. George jumped off the platform and plunged into the crowd. Men with drawn swords shepherded the king, the queen, Victoria and Gina away from the platform and into a small room just off the hall. They were locked in with several guards in the room, and a strong line of soldiers outside.

"Who is this?" the queen asked Victoria.

"This is my new friend, Regina, just in from the country," Victoria said.

"What country?" the king asked in a voice deep with concern. Gina couldn't think of an answer. She could hear brawling and clashing swords outside the door and she was afraid they'd send her away. The door burst open and a fierce looking man addressed the king.

"May I speak?" he asked the king.

"Of course, captain," the king answered.

"One of George's men is very drunk and has proclaimed that they have come to claim half your kingdom. That's what started the brawl. There may be nothing to it, but we must take it seriously. My men will clear the hall soon, but then you must submit to being guarded at all times, all of you. There are many ways your brother might go about claiming what he declares is his. You must order him to take up residence at Foxborough, and take all his people with him."

Suddenly the fierce eyes stared at Gina. "Who is this?" he barked.

"My friend," Victoria said, not at all threatened by the powerful captain of her father's huge army.

"She doesn't belong here. Come with me," he ordered.

"No!" Victoria stamped her foot, but the captain seized Gina by the shoulder and marched her to the door.

"No! No!" Victoria screamed. "No! No! Gina! Oh Gina. . . ."

Gina sat up in bed, the scene vivid in her mind. Her shoulder still hurt from the captain's grip. I didn't make up that whole castle and all those people and that fight. What do I know of such things? The story seems to come alive somehow. She only had to open her mind and it went on. She put her head down on the pillow.

If word spread to the continent of fighting between the king and his brother in Warwick, then the King of Lancaster and his son would quickly return and bring Justin back with them. The two armies together would surely defeat George and get rid of him. Justin would surely be a hero and . . .

She went fast asleep.

On Sundays, summer and winter, a carillon concert floated over the campus early in the morning. Instead of striking the hours, the bells pealed out in lovely classical music and hymns. The sound woke Gina. It would be a strange Sunday without David, she thought sadly. He made Sundays so joyful. He usually served his own brand of French toast to the family, tying an apron over the pants of his Sunday suit.

Her mother and Gina took turns going to church with him. Gina was very happy to go with him. Both before and after the service people would surround him, eager to talk with him.

This morning there would be no French toast. Her mother was making Instant Cream of Wheat in a saucer for Beth.

"I never could make French toast, Gina. Sorry," her mother said. "I know your father would like for you to go to church this morning. He'll want to know what the dean says about the lessons."

"I've never been there without him."

"I know, but it's good for you. I wish you could get to know some people your own age."

"Everybody here is either a professor or a college student. That's just the way it is."

"It won't be long before you're a college student."

"Two whole years . . . that's long. Before we came here I had so many hopes for my junior year. Now I may not even get to go back to Hansford High."

"It's got to work out somehow. We've got to believe whatever happens is for the best." Her mother gave her a quick hug and then said, "Scoot! Go get dressed."

She put on a green silk dress she had worn to her graduation from junior high. She walked to the chapel. Quite a lot of people walking on the gravel paths with her made her think of people in the Bible going to the Temple, or the people in England and Europe going to their cathedrals.

She climbed the steep stone steps, to the heavy red doors set in arched splendor. The organ was playing quietly. The atmosphere was hushed and expectant. She had to walk halfway down the aisle before she could find a seat. A cheerful looking older woman made room for her, sliding over and smiling.

Gina looked up at the vaulted ceiling high above

her head and then at the breathtaking stained glass windows. Ruby red and emerald green and bright blue against sparkling silver, pictures of the saints and angels looked down at her. Sitting alone she realized that when she was with her father she didn't notice the windows. People were always greeting him, speaking softly, shaking his hand.

Now she looked very carefully and tried to remember the story each window was telling. These were saints and angels from another world. These were people's stories that taught important lessons. She remembered a talk her father had given back in church at Hansford about whether there really were such people as Abraham or Sarah, or whether they were story people, loved and told about through long years. Did someone make up those stories, like her story for Beth?

The organ began the opening hymn. The people stood up and the choir came singing down the aisle. They had bright blue stoles and snowy white choir robes. The two ministers wore doctoral gowns, one with a bright orange silk hood down his back and the other with soft blue. The procession gave Gina a tingle of excitement. Then the solemnity of the service began. She listened very carefully. When a psalm was read responsively, the sound of so many people reading scripture together surrounded her. It made her feel part of something that flowed like a great river, carrying her along. Then the minister began to pray, and Gina found herself looking up at the window picturing John and Jesus at his baptism, a dove descending from a brilliant sky. It gave her the very strong sense that the person to whom they were praying was right there.

A lady read the story of Nicodemus from the Gospel of John in a pleasant, clear voice. Then the dean of the chapel climbed the steps to the pulpit. He adjusted the microphone in front of him briefly and then he began to speak.

"In this chapel this morning there are worlds of knowledge," he began, and the people settled themselves to listen.

"I mean the worlds you live in as members of the York community. There are the worlds of science, math, astronomy, physics and chemistry. There is the world of medicine, healing and curing, and a close association with death. Some of you live in the world of the arts, of painting and sculpture, music and dance and drama, and the world of story tellers. In the gospel today Jesus is talking about the world of the spirit."

Someone behind Gina coughed and coughed again.

"We talk about free spirits," the dean continued, "and so they are, but the ones I know deliberately choose to be spirit people. They search the scriptures for understanding. They do a lot of thinking about what it means. They pray and open themselves to God intentionally." The coughing started again. Someone got up and moved quickly down the aisle. Gina couldn't hear what the dean said next. Then he said, "I repeat, there is one such shining spirit among us here at York this summer. Most of you have heard of him by now, I'm sure. His name is David Worthington, and tomorrow morning he's going to be on national television. Before he left he said to me, 'what can I say in four minutes about a book it took me two years to write?'"

There was a ripple of amusement.

"Catch the Morning Show if you can, but more important, read his book, *Journey Into Light*. I have invited him to take my place next week. He is a gifted preacher. He is a spirit person, at home in the world Jesus speaks about, the world into which we are born, not of flesh, but intentionally, of the Spirit."

Gina held her breath. She had never expected to hear about her own father this morning. She thought about him being a spirit person. She knew he studied a lot, read a lot, wrote a lot, taught a lot. Ever since she could remember he had led the family in prayer, always in a way that told her how important it was to him, but also that he loved to do it.

"I hope," the dean was saying, "that he can become a permanent member of our community and that you, each of you, can get to know him. He is truly an inspiration, one of the most intelligent, creative people I have ever met. His book is full of imagination as well as clear logic. For him the focus is just as clear in the spirit world as it is in the world of the flesh, perhaps even more clear. How did he get this way? Because he works at it. That is what we must all think about this morning."

Gina kept listening, but she really didn't hear the rest of the sermon. She could feel a glow inside her, a glow of happiness. More than anyone in this big place full of people, she knew David Worthington. She belonged to him, he belonged to her. She was full of love and excitement.

When the service was over the lady who had made room for her said, "Aren't you David Worthington's daughter?"

Gina blushed with pleasure. "Yes."

"Come, let me introduce you to the dean."

He was standing in the door of the chapel, shaking hands with everyone, laughing and talking. He looked splendid in his robe trimmed with blue velvet ribbon on the sleeves and down the front. On his back the light blue hood seemed elegant indeed. When the lady introduced her, his face lit up. He took her hand in his, and stood there looking down at her, not saying a word for a moment. Then he said, "Of course I know you, Gina. You have your father's wonderful bright eyes!"

His smile and his hand were so warm, everything about him made her feel special.

"When is he coming home?"

"Tonight."

53

"I'll be glad when he's back. New York can be a rough place for gentle people. Tell him to come and tell me all about it as soon as he can."

"Yes, sir," Gina whispered and the dean turned to the next person waiting to speak to him.

All excited, Gina ran home. Julia was in the kitchen, standing at the stove.

"Did you know David is going to preach at the chapel next Sunday?" Gina burst out.

"He didn't tell me, but that's really nice."

"Could Mrs. Turner stay with Beth so we could both go?"

"We'll see, dear."

"And the dean said he hoped David would be a permanent member of the York community."

Her mother stopped stirring the chocolate pudding. She turned to Gina with wide eyes. "Really?"

"Yes. And he said everyone should read David's book."

"He said that . . . in his sermon?"

"Yes. It was about spirit people."

"I see." She turned back to the pudding, stirring in slow circles, absentmindedly.

"Would you want to stay here, Gina?" she asked.

Gina sat down at the kitchen table, still in her church dress.

"We have to stay until Beth is better," she said, but thinking beyond that. "There's something about this place that's . . . well, I love it. It's kind of mysterious. But I always thought I'd graduate from Hansford High with my friends . . . Elsie and Fiona, all the ones I've always known."

Her mother took the pudding off the stove and poured it, steaming, into crystal dishes.

"Our house at Hansford, the people at church, the way everybody in town knows each other, all that would be hard for me to leave," Julia said.

She opened a bag of marshmallows and put one in each dish where they promptly began to melt into sweet topping.

"Julia," Gina said, getting up slowly, "it really doesn't matter. I could be happy either place, as long as we're together. I hate it when David is gone."

"So do I," her mother said with a big sigh. "So do I."

CHAPTER FOUR
Storms and Anxiety

After lunch the sky was full of dark clouds and a gusty wind began to blow. It was cooler than it had been all week. Gina put a lacy shawl around Beth's shoulders. It alarmed her that Beth looked unhappy. "What's wrong?" she asked.

"Something's got to happen to the princess. You just can't leave her all sad and lonely. There's got to be more to the story."

"There is," Gina assured her, "Only I didn't make it up, it happened."

"Wow!" Beth said with a little bounce. "Tell me."

So Gina told her about the Great Hall with the fires burning, the torches flaming, the mountains of food and the dogs everywhere. She told about the king's brother, George, and the men getting drunk and fighting, and the way the captain forced her out of the room. She could still hear Victoria calling her name, "Gina, oh Gina!"

"George is evil, Beth," Gina said.

"What is evil?" Beth asked, "What does that mean?"

"Bad. Wrong. Hurtful," Gina said. She could see George sitting next to the king. She could see the captain, feel his grip on her shoulder. "I was in the Great Hall of the castle. There was a feast to celebrate the return of the king's brother. I saw Victoria and the king and the queen. I talked to them and they talked to me."

"You didn't make this up just to tell me? You were there? I want to believe you, Gina, but how could this happen?"

"It's as though Victoria and the king and the queen are real people."

"And George is bad and wrong?"

"He's going to hurt people."

"Victoria?" Beth shuddered.

"I'm afraid so, and the only person I know to save her is . . ."

"Justin," Beth finished.

"Only he's gone, like David." Gina sighed. "Maybe word will get to Henry's father about George and they will come back to help. But I just don't know."

"Oh my," Beth said with a sort of a wail. Gina sat down on the bed and picked up Beth's hand. "Let's forget about the story for a while. I'll think of a happy ending, I don't want you worrying. Let me tell you what the dean of the chapel said this morning about David. He said he's one of the nicest people he's ever known, and he hopes we will stay here."

"Do you like it here, Gina? Better than home?"

"Well, maybe not better, but I do like it. The gardens especially. Let me get Mrs. Turner's book."

She read a little bit to Beth about how formal gardens have carefully considered master plans before they are even begun. They looked at the pictures of fountains and statues and trees and shrubs and acres of flowers.

"This is an Italian garden," Gina explained, "in Giordani, Italy, it says."

"Is that where Justin and Henry are?"

"Beth, listen. It's make-believe, the story. Forget about it."

"I can't forget it. You said it seemed real to you. It seems real to me. What ever will happen to Victoria?"

Just then a rumble of thunder invaded the room. Outside the window even stronger wind began to blow. The curtains in the open window flapped wildly. A flash of lightning flickered and a loud clap of thunder followed. Julia flew into the room, closed the open window and looked at her watch.

"Let's hope it goes away," she said. "This is not good weather for flying."

Rain slashed against the window glass as if

someone had thrown a bucket of water at it. Julia turned on a light on the table by Beth's bed just as another huge sound of thunder seemed to surround them, all around and even underneath them.

"Mama!" Beth cried out. Julia sat down beside her and took her in her arms, rocked her back and forth, gently.

"It's just a summer storm, dearie. It won't last long."

The light started to flicker and then went out. There was a roar of high wind and the sound of pelting rain. Gina sat on the floor beside her mother, leaning her head against her leg.

"What time is the plane?"

"Not for two hours, but the problem is, there's a whole band of these storms coming, one right after the other according to the TV. Some of them severe, they say."

Far away in the distance they heard a siren. The next clap of thunder seemed to rattle the whole room. Then, as quickly as it had come, the storm stopped. The lights went back on and everything was quiet. Gina got up and looked out the window. There were puddles everywhere. The trees were dripping; the sky was still unusually black. There was no one in sight.

Time dragged on. Gina brought the portable TV into Beth's room, and they found some cartoons to amuse her. Julia went back to work. Gina went to her room, curled up on her bed.

She was only half awake when she heard a siren again, louder than before, and seeming to come closer and closer. It sounded scary to Gina. She sat up. She heard a voice, and thought it was Beth's TV. Then she heard the voice calling her own name.

"Help me, Gina! Help me!"

Gina knew it was Victoria's voice. She knew Victoria was terrified. She tried to answer, but no sound came out. Ice cold fear took hold of her. Victoria screamed, and Gina's heart stopped. She couldn't breathe. The siren was very close now and very loud.

"Someone's in bad trouble," her mother said, standing in the doorway. "It's a terrible sound, isn't it?"

Then she looked more closely at Gina and said, "Are you all right?"

"I don't know," Gina heard herself say. "I don't know."

"You're so pale, what is it?"

"I guess it's just the storm."

The ambulance rolled by heavily, on its way to the hospital.

"I can't remember time standing still the way it has today." Julia crossed the room, stood looking down at Gina. "I may never let your father out of my sight again."

Gina smiled. "We count on him, don't we? We really need him."

They heard a little scratching at the window. It

had begun to rain again.

Julia said, "We better go look at cartoons. Let's hope they're funny."

"I'll come in a minute." Gina got up off the bed. She ran some cold water in the bathroom sink and dashed it on her face.

Somehow she felt hot, now, almost feverish. She reached for a towel and buried her face in it, and as she did she heard a very faint voice, quiet now, pitifully say, "Help me, Gina."

"What can I do?" she said, out loud.

"Find Justin. You have to find Justin."

"How?" she asked. There was no answer.

Suddenly, it seemed to her that she had to get out of the house to think. She got an umbrella out of her closet and went to Beth's room. "I'm going for a quick walk to get some fresh air. I won't be long."

"Hurry back if it starts to thunder again," her mother said.

The rain was not heavy, the air was slightly foggy, the wind wasn't blowing as she walked along.

"Imagination," she thought to herself, "that's what the dean said David has, great imagination. Mine is getting the better of me. I have to make a strong effort not to go on with this crazy business."

She decided to go straight to the chapel. She could sit quietly out of the rain and think. It was as though she were being pushed along, she was so anxious to get there. The campus was deserted, normal for a Sunday evening. Students were either in their rooms or off campus in town. Alone, she climbed the steps and pulled at the heavy red-colored door. To her dismay it was firmly locked. She remembered a side door where her father often took her when he was in a hurry to get home from service.

She found it, and it was not locked. Inside it was dark and she wasn't sure which way to go. She came to another door, and when she opened it, she was standing close to the front of the chapel. For a moment the beauty of it overwhelmed her. The great shining cross on the high altar gleamed in the half dark. The light through the stained glass windows made her feel as if she were underwater, in a pure blue atmosphere. Slowly she sank down on a soft red velvet cushion in a side pew.

"Even if I made up my mind to find Justin I couldn't do it," she told herself. "If I tell anyone I hear voices and a beautiful princess needs me they'll think I'm sick. What am I to do? I'm the one who needs help. I think I'm going out of my mind."

Instinctively, in that place she looked up. In this light she couldn't see the saints and angels. She closed her eyes. She sat in the deep silence.

And then she felt someone was near her. She opened her eyes, and Justin was standing there. He was dressed in a leather belted brown tunic, brown stockings and boots. His hair was dark and curly. His eyes were dark too, as he stared at her.

"Who are you?" he asked in a whisper that seemed to hang in the air between them.

"I'm Gina. Are you Justin?"

"I am," he answered, "and I have no idea where I am or why."

"Victoria is in trouble. She needs you, she begged me to tell you. I thought you were still in Italy."

"No, Henry and his father are only one night away from Warwick. We heard about George's plot against his brother. We traveled night and day to get there. We had to rest and decide what to do. I was so tired and worried I couldn't sleep." He looked all around the chapel, then up at the windows. "What is this place?"

"It's York Chapel."

"I know of no York Chapel."

"It's in a different time, in a different place, far from England."

"How do you know that Victoria's in trouble?"

"I heard her voice."

"I must be dreaming."

Gina reached out and touched his arm. "You're real, and you're with me in this chapel right now."

He put his hand over hers. He said, "You're right. What do we do now?"

Gina stood up and realized how tall he was, and that he was as handsome as anyone she had ever seen.

"I know it was Victoria's voice, Justin. I don't know how it happened, but I was there when a fight broke out. I know that George wants half of his brother's kingdom."

"Half?" Justin gave a quick shake of his head. "What can he possibly have to force such an agreement?"

"Oh, Justin! That's it!" Everything suddenly became clear to Gina. "That's surely it! He has Victoria!"

Justin put both hands on her shoulders, looked deep into her eyes, still as a statue for a moment.

"On my oath," he said softly, "you may be right."

Above their heads there was a flash of lightning and then a low growl of thunder.

"This place," he said, sliding his hand down to hold hers, "I somehow feel I know it. It's familiar to me."

He looked up at the windows. "What did you say . . . ?"

"York University Chapel."

"Where?"

"In America, Justin."

"America? And you can hear Victoria's voice?"

"Yes."

"Why?" He found her other hand.

"Because I created her, in a story I was making up for my little sister who is sick. And I created you, too."

Justin looked at her in disbelief. "No, I don't think so," he said. "Our world is there. Somehow you found us."

65

"She's in trouble. She told me to find you, and somehow I did. Will you go back to help her?"

"I must, of course."

There was a brilliant flash of lightning and the roar of thunder that followed it filled the chapel with rolling sound.

As it died away, Justin said, "Whoever is in command of all this surely chose a lovely person to help me."

The chapel was full of lightning and thunder at the same time, dazzling lightning, deafening thunder. Gina put her hands over her ears. In a few seconds it was still again, and Justin was gone.

She found her umbrella under the pew and the door at the side of the chapel. Outside the rain was heavy and the wind was blowing hard again. In no time she was soaked through. Her umbrella was fighting to pull loose from her hand. She began to sob, tears running down her cheeks, and she didn't know why.

"God," she prayed, "Please help us."

Julia was standing in the doorway when she reached the apartment. "It couldn't be worse. I didn't know where you were . . . I couldn't leave to look for you . . . the plane is due any minute . . . and here's this awful storm."

If I told you what just happened to me, you might think it could be worse, she thought, because what is happening in Warwick is happening to me. It isn't over. It won't be over until all the stress, all the chaos in Warwick is resolved. When that would be, when it could be, there is no way of knowing. But the words "a lovely person" seemed like a sweet smelling bouquet to her. His sensitive face, his warm fingers and his tall strength; she tried to keep all of it close to her. He's as real as I am, she told herself.

"Where were you?" her mother asked.

"In the chapel until the storm scared me, and I came home."

"Do you think they can possibly land with all this turbulence, Gina? Oh, how I wish he would call and say the flight was canceled, and he's safe in New York, that he will come home tomorrow. But you're drenched. Go take a hot bath, child. Soak yourself in a hot bath, and maybe by the time you're warm he'll be here."

There were still rumbles of thunder and flickers of lightning, as she eased herself into the tub. It was hot and steamy. It felt soothing to her body, but her mind was racing.

If she were to tell the whole story carefully and calmly to her father, would he be able to tell her what had happened? What could have happened? Was it her imagination, out of control?

She sank down under the water, felt the water soak her hair, closed her eyes and thought about Justin. Wherever in the world was he now? She listened, half expecting to hear voices again, but there were none. Silence, only silence, and warm water supporting her. It seemed to her, however, that the silence was affirming.

She pulled out the plug, let the water drain out, got out of the tub and rubbed her hair vigorously with a big towel. She put on a flowered nightgown, a bathrobe to match, tied the ribbon at her throat. She heard the front door open and her mother's joyful cry.

"David! Oh, David! You're home!"

She flew down the stairs and joined their embrace. A great surge of happiness swept over her to feel him, his coat as wet as her hair, with his arm around her, holding her close to him.

CHAPTER FIVE
Fame and Misfortunes

"It was unbelievable," he said after he'd had a shower and a sandwich, and they had assured him that Beth was doing well. "Everyone I met up there was full of energy and electricity, but somehow seemed driven, kind of out of control. Even Eliot seemed to get caught up in it. There was a set-up in the studio where I and this slick looking anchor man sat toe to toe in motel-type chairs. They asked me if I wanted to put what I'd say on a TelePrompTer, but I said I really would rather just answer the questions as they came. Teaching, I do that all the time."

He laughed, rubbed his chin. "They looked at me funny, and I know they thought when all the bright lights were turned on, when the cameras, pointed at us like cannons, were turned on and the red lights flared, I'd panic. Just before time to begin, a flustered woman came and attacked my necktie. Imagine! She ripped it off, said it was a terrible color, and with the most awful spidery fingers she knotted another one tight around my neck. I loosened it carefully, thinking, 'these poor, driven people. I have something to offer you. I can tell you about peace, joy, love.'"

Julia filled his cup with steaming coffee and put a loving hand on his shoulder. He covered her hand with his, and it made Gina think of how Justin had done just that.

"So it went well?" Julia asked.

"Yes. There is more, I must tell you." He pulled folded sheets of paper out of his pocket and spread them on the table. "This is an offer the publishers have made to Eliot and me. They want me to take a year off from teaching. They want me to tour the whole country. Here's a list of places already wanting me to come and talk about the book. There's an invitation to be part of a seminar at a school I have admired for years."

"But David . . ." Julia began, then stopped.

"I know," he said. "Beth."

"When summer school is over, we can't stay here. This apartment belongs to regular faculty."

"There's more," David said, "They are offering me twice as much money as I make now. This tour stuff will be only a few months at a time. In between they want me to write another book. Eliot would be editing again."

David shuffled the papers, put them into a neat pile.

"Maybe we could find another apartment in this town. That way, Beth would be near the medical center and finish her therapy. You'd be safe here, wouldn't you?"

They were all three very quiet. Then Gina said. "You're home. That's all that matters. What time is the interview?"

"Just before eight. I'll set an alarm."

She went upstairs to bed but not to sleep. She heard them talking late into the night.

They needed no alarm clock to wake them. They were up early. Beth and David spent some quiet time together while Gina and Julia made quick work of breakfast. Gina took Beth's tray up to her and David turned on the portable TV in her room. Julia helped Beth to sit up.

"The news desk is nowhere near as large as it looks in that picture," he said. "The whole place is full of lights and cameras and cables and wires and voices coming out of the control room. It's a wonder to me that anyone can make sense, let alone be perfectly groomed and smiling."

"It's going to be funny," Beth said, "you being here with us and seeing you there. People can't be two places at once."

"Illusion," David said.

"What's that?" Beth wanted to know.

71

"Seeing something that isn't real."

In a flash Gina saw the blue light in the chapel, and felt Justin's warm touch. "What's really real?" she said, without thinking. Her father turned to her with great question in his eyes. He always knew when Gina was serious.

"Really real?" He hesitated.

"That's all the news for now," the TV said. "Let's switch to weather central."

"Let me think about that," David said. "The interview comes on right after the weather." Gina wished she hadn't spoken.

Beth, her chin resting on her drawn up knees, her eyes bright as stars, sat waiting breathlessly. Her mother and father sitting by the window, holding hands, stared at the little set. Only Gina wasn't completely absorbed. She kept thinking, "What is real?"

"Here we go," David said.

There was a picture of a man sitting in a chair that tipped him back. He spoke with a smile as if he were about to introduce a child, or a pet.

"Books about religion don't usually hit the best seller list within a few weeks of publication," he said, "yet that is what has happened to David Worthington's book, *Journey Into Light*. I want to introduce him to you this morning to tell us why he thinks this has happened. David Worthington."

The camera switched to a picture of David, sitting up very straight, his face lit up with pure pleasure. Everything about him seemed to glow.

"Tell us what you think, David."

"I think it's because I've been given a message of hope. It seems to me a lot of people today are not happy. Some are driven by ambition, by competition, by demanding jobs or demanding bosses. Some are lonely; loneliness can hurt. For some, life has gotten flat, the world seems grim."

"Because they don't have faith?" The interviewer, Roy, wanted him to get on with religion. "As I see it, very few people today want to take that leap of faith into the dark, into the unknown."

"A favorite image of mine is that of the Good Shepherd," David said. "My faith tells me that rather than leaping into the dark, as you put it, we are invited to follow a shepherd we can trust with our very lives. He can lead us through anything we have to face. He can show us the way. There is nothing we have to face that he hasn't faced himself. He is one of us, yet he is the Son of God."

"That's a pretty picture, like Bible stories for children. But our viewers don't think in terms of being sheep or following a shepherd. In the book you outline steps for religious discipline. Talk about them."

David made a little tent of his two hands, held them against his mouth, closed his eyes for a brief second. Then he spoke.

"I do make some suggestions about spirituality.

But really, Roy, what I have written is not a self-help manual, with steps to improve yourself. It's about a journey and some observations for fellow travelers."

"So where is this journey going?"

"Into the spirit world. Into a relationship with our Lord."

"Ah," Roy smiled an icy smile. "And you make it sound so joyful, so fulfilling, so wonderful that people everywhere are wanting to begin the journey. Is that how you see it?" He seemed to be saying that he didn't think such a thing could be possible.

Gina thought if someone talked to me like that, I'd get mad. But her father didn't seem to hear the ridicule.

"Exactly," he said with a great grin. "I guarantee it. There's a freedom in it that is marvelous. It's like being let out of a dark closet into a spring day. It's like leaving all your doubts and fears behind you and being perfectly sure you can do whatever you really want to do."

"How do I get in on this?" Still the icy smile.

"Accept it. It's a gift already given. You are loved." There was a lovely sparkle in David's eyes as he spoke directly to Roy. The camera moved in close to focus on both of them.

"Loved?" Roy shifted uncomfortably in his chair, straightened up a little.

"Yes. You know the verse they always hold up in the end zone at football games, hoping the camera will pick it up along with the extra point after touchdown. 'God so loved the world that he gave...' God isn't something vague, not a theory made up by men. He loves the world he created, and he did something about saving it from self-destruction. He gave. That's a specific act, in a specific time and space, a historical fact. The saving process is still going on, offered to each one of us. It's offered to nations and peoples everywhere."

"Well, we're out of time, my friend," Roy said. "Thank you very much."

There was a blast of music, a shot of the program logo and then a cough syrup commercial.

David stood up and turned off the set. "They cut it," he said, "but before Eliot and I got out of the studio, a voice told me not to leave. The director wanted to speak to me. I waited, and Eliot fidgeted, worried we were going to have to do the whole thing over again."

"I thought it was perfect," Gina burst out. "You looked great, what you said was great. It couldn't have been better."

"What he wanted was for me to tape a longer interview to run on an evening show with someone called Peter Ames, who does what they call 'essays'. The director was upset with Roy. He said Roy was much too 'flip', as he called it. He said he thought it would be really good to do a more 'in-depth' interview."

"Did you do it?" Beth asked.

"I did. Peter Ames is one of the most interesting men I've ever met. We were friends at once. He suggested we just sit down and talk with the cameras running, without any time restrictions. We talked, all right, enough for two shows, it turns out. The first one airs next week, and then another one after that.

"Eliot must have been thrilled," Julia said with a laugh.

"He was. Like a child. But for him, the best part was when we walked out of that great skyscraper, and there were almost a dozen reporters, guys with hand microphones, waiting for us. We were on the evening news as well."

"What brought the reporters?" Julia was excited.

"They had a report that my book had sold out all over the city and that I was in town for the broadcast."

"You were good, David. There's something about you when you talk . . . it's as much how you look as what you say . . . it's magic!"

David looked at his watch. "Wow!" he said, "It'll take magic to get me to class on time. 'Bye! See you at lunch."

"Before you go, write in Mrs. Turner's book?"

"Sure," he said. "I'll be in my studio."

Gina ran to her room, grabbed the book off the dresser and hurried downstairs. David was putting test papers in a briefcase. He sat down and reached for a pen.

"She's the nurse you and Beth like so much?" he asked.

Gina nodded. "She's really nice. She loved your book, and she wants to send it to her son. His name is Kevin Turner."

He wrote carefully, concentrating. Then he gave Gina the book, "How's that?"

She read, "To Kevin: Join our band of travelers on the way to becoming. Peace! David Worthington."

"Perfect!" Gina said happily.

"I haven't forgotten your question, Gina dear. I'll try to get home for lunch."

Beth pushed her untouched breakfast away from her. Gina took the tray and put it on the dresser.

"I'm just so awfully tired of this," Beth said.

"You're not hungry? Too much excitement, I guess, for all of us." Gina put her hand on Beth's forehead. She seemed to be okay.

"No, that's not it." Beth put a little accent of impatience on every word. "I'm tired of this room. I'm tired of this bed. I'm tired of being tired. It's the story, too. I want it to come to the happy ending. I want you to make it come out right. You started it, finish it!"

"Maybe I could do that," Gina said as much to herself as to Beth. "You're right. It is my creation."

"Well then, begin the end."

77

"I have to think. I'll take your tray down and be right back."

Gina picked up the tray and while she was going to the kitchen she reviewed in her mind where she had actually left the story. Putting everything together she had Victoria kidnapped and held for ransom in some unknown place. Where might that be? Little thatched huts of the common people were all around the castle. It had to be one of them, isolated, defendable. It had to be George who had done this. If he demanded that King Richard come alone to retrieve his daughter then the king could be killed. But that would never happen. Some plan would be made to protect the king at all costs.

Gina leaned against the sink and rinsed Beth's dishes in warm water. There would be no windows in the little hut. It would be quite dark inside. Victoria would be tied up. There would surely be a heavily armed guard. Soldiers would surround the hut, and maybe there would be an old woman to look after Victoria.

For no logical reason Gina thought about the fragrance of the wisteria in the garden. Victoria might smell grapes and know that the hut is hidden in the forest bordering the vineyards.

There must be some way I can end this story and forget about it, she told herself. She knew perfectly well, however, that she didn't want to forget about it. Most of all she didn't want to forget about Justin.

Halfway up the stairs to Beth's room she heard Mrs. Turner knocking on the door. Good, she thought, that will give me a little more time to figure this out.

She was happy to see Mrs. Turner, and happy to give her the autographed book.

"Oh, this is wonderful, Gina! Thank you, thank you!"

But the cheerfulness and the happiness dissolved a few minutes later as Mrs. Turner examined Beth. Gina knew at once that something was wrong.

Mrs. Turner looked very serious, doing the usual routine. Then, instead of putting all the instruments back in her bag, she went through the whole thing again. She took a notebook out of her bag and wrote in it after each test.

Downstairs, Mrs. Turner asked if anything had upset Beth. Gina told her about the interview on TV. "It couldn't have upset her, though. She loved it. We all knew it was a great success. The storm last night, though, and all of us worrying about David flying home, maybe that was it."

"She seems listless to me and all her vitals reflect that. I think I must ask Dr. Gates to check her, just to be sure."

"She's been doing so well." Gina felt sick.

"It happens in cases like this. We don't know why. Recovery isn't always steady. Keep a close eye on her. Call me if you notice anything unusual."

Upstairs, Beth was in a bad mood. "I'm glad she's gone," she said, a frown on her face. "What was the matter with her this morning?"

"She's decided Dr. Gates should look at you. She was getting all the details together for him. They do that all the time at the hospital."

Beth lay flat in the bed with her eyes closed.

"I'm so tired of all this. Please, Gina, finish the story with a happy ending, that will help me."

"I think I've got it," Gina said. "Listen."

This has to be simple, she told herself. No more problems, no more crisis. She began, "By the time the King of Lancaster, Henry's father, and all his company reached Warwick, the kidnapping of the princess was stunning news. George and his men had left the castle and gone to his estate, Foxborough. He had taken with him the captain of King Richard's men. Then came a ransom note to the king, saying that George was holding the princess. He would release her only if an agreement was made that Richard would split his kingdom in two, giving half to George. He must bring this agreement, ready to sign, to the Great Hall the following day if he ever wanted to see his daughter again."

Gina stopped to think. What would the king do? Well, he must try to find the hut.

"Justin and Henry and all the king's men rode all over the countryside looking for a hut with a guard around it," she went on. "Justin and Henry found it, in the forest at the edge of the vineyard. They rode like the wind to tell the King and Justin's father.

"'How would it be,' Justin asked his father, 'if Henry and I waited until the guards were asleep, just before dawn, and then slipped in and got Victoria? If we had to fight we can take care of ourselves, but if we do it right, they'll never know until morning.'

"'It's too dangerous,' his father told him. 'Henry is a king's son, and you are my only son. No, I can't let you do it.'

"'Ask the king,' Justin insisted.

"So he and his father went to King Richard who listened with a grim face while Justin told him of the plan. Richard sent for Henry's father who was staying in the castle, and he listened as Justin went through it all again. He asked questions about how many men there were and how many horses. He asked about the hut and shook his head when Justin told him it had only one door and no windows.

"'The inside of that hut will be black as pitch. You couldn't even see the princess.'

"'It might take some time to do it, but I think I could.'

"'You couldn't make one bit of sound.'

"'I know, but sir, what are the alternatives? If

you take a company to fight them, they probably have orders to kill Victoria.'

"The king made a strangled sound, (Gina was getting really into the story now.)

"'I have a small company of men I have known and trusted for twenty years,' Justin's father said. 'We have done night missions like this one successfully. If the boys can get the princess out, say into the woods, then we can carry out a surprise attack, protecting all three of them.'

"'I can't agree,' King Richard sounded sad. 'I can't put your sons at risk.'

"'Richard, have you a better plan?' Henry's father asked."

Beth sat up in the bed. She was not pleased.

"So Justin and Henry rescue Victoria, Henry marries her, and they all live happily ever after?" Beth said, pouting. "What about Justin?"

The doorbell rang, startling them both.

Gina hurried downstairs, opened the door and there was Dr. Gates. The size of him took Gina by surprise. He towered over her. She had seen him at the hospital during those terrible days, but now, close to her, he was frightening.

"I'm Dr. Gates," he said. "You're Beth's sister?"

Gina nodded and said, "Please come in."

He walked in, looking very serious. He followed Gina up the stairs.

"Well, young lady," he said to Beth, who looked scared, "let's see what's going on."

That was all he said. He did the same routine that Mrs. Turner did. Gina found herself hardly able to breathe. Beth seemed suddenly limp like a little doll, letting the doctor do whatever he wanted. There was silence in the room.

Then the doctor said, "Where are your parents?"

"My mother is an assistant to Dr. Glover in the art building, and my father is teaching at Stuyvesant Hall."

Dr. Gates took the stethoscope off his neck and folded it carefully into his bag.

"Let's get one of them here as quickly as we can."

Beth started to cry. Gina went to her and put her arms around her.

"What is it?" Gina said to the doctor.

"We need to do some tests just as fast as we can. It may be nothing, but I can't take a chance. Would you like me to call your mother?"

"Yes," Gina said, "the number is right there by the phone downstairs in the kitchen."

"Pack a suitcase for her, enough to stay two or three days." It was a command, not a suggestion.

"I'm so scared," Beth said in a very small voice as he went down to the kitchen. "I don't want to go back to the hospital. Those tests they do are really horrible. I want to be here with you, just you, Gina."

"Have you been feeling not so good, Beth?"

"I was worried about Victoria . . ."

"Oh Beth! Then it's my fault! I did this to you!

I'm so sorry!"

"You finished the story, but I don't think it's over."

"I'm never going to think about it again. Not ever!"

"I bet you can't help it, Gina."

Gina went to the closet and got out a suitcase that brought back memories of following the speeding ambulance to the medical center from Hansford.

She packed a bathrobe and slippers from the closet and little nightgowns from the dresser drawer. All the time she was doing this she was feeling full of guilt, feeling as if she had done something very wrong.

Her mother and the ambulance arrived at the same time. The ambulance pulled up quietly at the curb. Two men brought a stretcher up to Beth's room. Gina had dressed her in a pretty pink dress with a ribbon in her hair. She looked as if she were going to a party, not to the hospital. Julia burst into tears.

Dr. Gates took two giant steps and caught her in his arms. The change in the man took Gina completely by surprise. His voice was so kind when he said, "Now please, Julia, don't be afraid. It's not really terribly threatening. I have to be sure it doesn't develop into trouble. I want her where we can watch her carefully." He held Julia's head against his shoulder, then let her go with a little hug.

Julia dashed her hand over her eyes, struggled to smile.

"Do I have to lie down?" Beth asked, looking at the two men.

"We'll carry you like a queen," one of the men said with a grin. He put two big pillows one on top of the other. He helped her lie against them so that she was halfway sitting up. "There," he said, "Don't you look pretty?"

They made a little procession down the stairs and out to the open doors of the ambulance.

"You stay here, Gina," Julia said. "If David calls or comes home, tell him what Dr. Gates said so he won't get upset the way I did."

So Gina watched the ambulance slowly drive away. Her mother and the doctor followed in his car. When she went back into the apartment and closed the door, the place seemed vastly empty. Without Beth, she thought, what shall I do?

Just to keep busy, she took the sheets off Beth's bed and put them in the hamper. She made the bed with fresh sheets, and when she had finished it looked even more strange with Beth gone.

She sat down in the chair by the window, looking out but not seeing anything. It was so awfully quiet.

The feeling of guilt kept coming back like acid

indigestion. She closed her mind to what had become a habit. She must not keep thinking about the story, about Victoria, the king and queen, Henry and his father, and Justin. She refused to think about them, she refused.

She thought about fixing some lunch for her father. Then she realized that lunch would be the last thing on his mind when she told him about Beth. The telephone rang. It was Eliot, and he was disappointed that David was out.

"Did you guys watch the interview?" he wanted to know.

"Yes, we did," Gina answered.

"Wasn't it great? Isn't he wonderful? It looks like he could run for President. Aren't you all thrilled about the contract?"

When she didn't answer, he said, "Gina? Is something wrong?"

"My sister . . . they took her to the hospital. I'm waiting for David to call or come home for lunch. He doesn't know yet."

"Is it serious?"

"I think so," Gina was just barely able to say it.

"Gee, I'm sorry," Eliot said. "What a bummer. Right now when everything is so exciting. Ask him to give me a call as soon as he can."

Gina forced herself to say, "I'll tell him."

"Listen, Gina, really . . . I hate this. Tell David you're all in my prayers."

"Thanks, Eliot," she said and hung up.

An hour later her father called, saying, "I can't get home for lunch. I'm supposed to see the dean right now. So many people showed up for my lecture this morning we had to turn them away. It's not fair to the students who have to pass this course. I need to make that clear. It's all very nice to have this open door policy, but not if it interferes with the students' rights."

"David," Gina said fearfully, knowing that what she must tell him would alarm him.

"I know. Your question . . ."

"It's not that. It's Beth. Dr. Gates was here this morning, and he has taken her to the hospital. He says it's not threatening but he thinks there may be something wrong. He wants to watch Beth closely. There are tests he wants to do."

Before she finished, he shouted, "Oh, my God! No!"

"Julia is there. Dr. Gates told us not to be afraid."

"I'll get over there fast. Are you all right?"

"I'm scared," she said.

"Me, too, Gina. Me, too."

The phone buzzed in her hand. She put it down carefully. The silence surrounded her again. Now the loneliness was darker, was deeper, was more in control of her than she could ever remember. She felt entirely alone, left out of everything. It was a kind of numbness starting in her arms and legs, taking over her whole body.

"I have to get out of this place," she decided. "I have to get myself straightened out. Exercise, that's what I need, mindless, hard exercise. I'll put on my sneakers and go run on the track." She was thinking of the track at Hansford College, but this was York University. She had no idea where the track was. So she decided just to go walk in the gardens.

It was lunch time, and the students were everywhere, enjoying the lovely summer day. Most of them had on shorts . There was an atmosphere of friendship and laughter. It made her feel even worse, for she had no part in it. Indeed, she wondered, did she have a part in anything? She jogged through the campus to the road leading to the medical center. She looked up at the top floor and wondered which room her family was in, and what was happening. She went on to the gardens, walking fast. She had not come to wander around enjoying the colors and the fragrance. She had come to get herself straight by exercising. She made herself go just as fast as she could.

By the time she got to the wisteria trellises she was out of breath. She sat down on a cool stone bench. She leaned forward and held her head in her hands. Don't cry in public for goodness sake, she told herself. What a baby you are. She bit her lip. Someone put a hand on her shoulder. Startled, she looked up. Incredibly, there stood Justin, dressed in blue knee britches and a silky white shirt.

"Justin!" she exclaimed.

"Gina!" his eyes danced. "I found you. I knew I could, I have no idea how. It's a kind of fascination I have for you. It's a kind of spell you have cast over me, or someone else has cast over us both."

He sat down beside her, picked up her hand in the most comforting and loving way.

"I think you know where they are keeping Victoria. I must find out where it is. We have searched the countryside. We cannot find the place. There is no time to waste."

"It's in the forest on the edge of the vineyard, at the very farthest end," Gina said, and was astonished that she said it. "I made that up, though, Justin, just to finish the story for my sister. I told her that an old woman is in the hut, guarding Victoria. I told her Victoria is tied to a bed with strong rope around her wrists and her ankles, tied to the bed post."

"It's no story, you know. Right now, it's happening. You have seen the place? Could you take me to it?"

"It has a thatched roof, it has no windows, it must be a vineyard worker's cottage."

Some students strolled by and looked with amusement at Justin. Gina realized he did look quite different, not conforming with the tee shirt and shorts uniform. He didn't take the slightest notice but gave her hand a little shake.

"How do you know this?" he asked.

"Justin, I made it up to entertain my little sister. And there is deep trouble in my world. She's sick again, and . . ."

"Is there anything you can do to help her?" Justin's question sounded urgent.

"No. I can pray, and I have surely done that."

"But you can help Victoria, don't you see? You can. If you can show us where she is, we can rescue her. We must rescue her. It's the captain of the king's army himself who is holding her. They want King Richard to agree to give George half his kingdom. It is a wicked plot. George has made the captain his chancellor. That is just what the scoundrel has always wanted. My father thinks he's as crooked as an old apple tree."

Gina looked at his earnest face.

"And you, Justin," she said, "you have always loved Victoria."

"Like a little sister. My whole family loves her."

"And Henry?"

"Yes, Henry does love her." He stood up. "I must hurry. Will you come with me and help Victoria?"

"How can I come with you? How can I help Victoria?"

He reached out a hand and pulled her up against him, folding his arms around her. He tipped up her chin and kissed her softly on the lips. "Come with me," he whispered and she closed her eyes and kissed him back.

When she opened her eyes, they were under a trellis of wisteria, the same delicious fragrance was in the air. There was a castle close by, standing upon a hill, turrets and towers, surrounded with deep, dark water. Stretching toward the horizon were the king's vineyards.

"Oh, glory! Oh, glory!" Justin fairly shouted and kissed her again, full of joy. "Come! I must take you to my mother."

"Why?" Gina asked as he pulled her along.

"To find proper clothes to cover you."

Gina realized she was wearing very short shorts and an old shapeless shirt, having come out not caring one bit how she looked. It was much cooler in this country, and it seemed the sun was about to go down. Justin led her across the drawbridge, up the stone steps, flight after flight. Finally, he knocked on an arched doorway. "It's Justin, let me in," he called.

The door opened a tiny crack; someone peered out. Then the door opened wide and they entered quickly. The heavy door shut behind them.

"This is my mother, Gina. Her name is Natalie. This is Gina, Mother, the girl I have told you about."

Natalie had her son's dark curly hair. She smiled at Gina.

"Welcome, Gina." They looked at each other, and they liked each other at once. Natalie stepped forward and hugged Gina. "Thank you for coming, my dear," she said, "You are as beautiful as my son has told me."

"Dressed as she is she will not be able to help us, Mother. Would any of Victoria's clothes fit her?"

"All of them, I think, but you will not want her to look like a princess."

"She looks like a princess to me no matter what," Justin said, "but there's one blue homespun dress I like. Can you find it for her?"

"Come and see," Natalie said to Gina. "Your real name is Regina?" Gina nodded. "That's a queen's name."

She took Gina into a room with a barred window looking out toward the high mountains. She found the blue dress made of what seemed like homespun linen, a soft blue, with a long skirt and a pretty neckline edged with lace. "Try this," she said.

Gina looked down at herself, knowing that all she had on underneath her shorts and blouse were cotton panties, nothing else. She was embarrassed.

"Oh." Natalie laughed, "This is what we need." Out of a drawer she pulled a fine linen petticoat with a low scooped neck and narrow lace shoulder straps. Gina stepped out of her shorts, pulled her old shirt over her head, and Natalie let the petticoat drop around her. Just the petticoat already made her feel good, but when they put the dress on her as well Natalie stepped back and admired her.

"Surely you are a princess, too, my dear. Surely you are."

The feel of the material was soft, luxurious. The way the skirt fit her narrow waist and fell in pleated folds to her ankles was lovely. She ran her fingers around the neckline of the bodice that fit her perfectly.

"Thank you," Gina said gratefully.

If Natalie had been pleased with the dress, Justin was, for a moment, overcome. He stood very still when he saw her.

"I have always loved that dress." he said. "I always knew it was special. I hope it will not attract too much attention."

"I have been here before, Justin. No one noticed me particularly."

"I don't understand." Justin looked puzzled.

"You were in Italy with Henry. I was here when the fight broke out in the Great Hall. I was with the king and the queen and Victoria when the captain locked them in a room."

"She was, dear," Natalie said. "I saw her with Victoria at the celebration." She turned to Gina. "She begged me to find you after they made you leave. I looked for you everywhere but I couldn't find you."

"The captain made me leave . . . I remember how mean he was."

"Mean, indeed," Justin smiled bitterly. "You have no idea how mean. We must find the hut where he is keeping Victoria."

"In my story . . ." Gina began.

"Forget about your story. This is real, this is serious. If you know what the place looks like we will search for it."

"How can you do that in daylight without being seen? If you search at night, how can you see?" Natalie said. "Besides, it's miles to the far end of the vineyards."

"The forest begins just beyond the green." Justin started pacing up and down the room. "We can walk tonight without being seen; there will be no moon. We can take the woodsmen's path that winds all through the forest. We'll know which hut it is because there will certainly be a guard posted. Since it's a cool night there will be a fire to warm them."

"Let me find Victoria's grey cloak. It will hide you and your pretty blonde hair." Natalie went to a closet and pulled out a cloak with a hood. She put it on Gina's shoulders, wrapped it around her, then put the hood over her head.

Both Natalie and Justin looked at her, lovingly. "What a beauty you are," Justin whispered. Gina reached out to Natalie, wanting to know that she was not dreaming, that Natalie's hand would be warm like her mother's. It was, and Gina's heart was joyful.

"Come, from the balcony outside this door we can look across to where we will go," Justin said. He held open the door for her, and they stepped out into the gathering twilight. They leaned against the chest high wall. To the right there was a high mountain range, blue in the evening shadow. Stretching out before them were two hundred yards of carpet green grass.

"There," Justin said, pointing a slender finger, "there's where the path leads into the woods. I've never followed it to the end. People don't like strangers in there."

He turned to Gina and smiled down at her. "You look so little in that cloak." He carefully pushed the hood back and touched her hair. "What a beauty you are," he said again, his eyes luminous.

"But you know," he said, "I don't dare kiss you. We might find ourselves back in your time, not mine!"

CHAPTER SIX
The Rescue

They walked, hand in hand, across the green, keeping far to the right of the castle. That way they reached the bordering forest quicker than any other way. There were guards looking down at them from their stations at the top of the castle, but it wasn't unusual for young couples to walk out together. A few insects hummed, the stars were brilliant. Even though the night was dark, soon Gina could see very well. With great relief they found the woodsmen's path and were enclosed in the welcome protecting shade of the thick woods. At first the path was wide and even, but then it got more and more narrow and rocky. They had walked quite a while when Justin stopped and listened. He pulled Gina off the path and into a thicket. She could hear the sound of a galloping horse not far away. In that quiet night it sounded like thunder as the rider sped by on the path.

"That's Kensington, I know him well. He's the captain's right hand man. I'll wager he's on his way to the hut. This must be the right path. It can't be too far."

The sound died away. The still night was restored. They started walking again. Sometimes there were big rocks in the path, and Justin reached out a steadying hand to help Gina climb over them. They walked a long time.

"Am I going too fast?" he asked. "Shall we rest?"

"Just let me catch my breath and think a little," Gina said.

"About what?" They found a mossy place and sat down, Justin leaned his back against a tree.

"You and Henry... how would you get her out of that hut, into the woods? There's an old woman in that hut guarding her as well as the men outside. They have her tied up with heavy rope, you'll have to cut it. It will be totally dark. Wouldn't that be terribly dangerous?"

"Not if we waited until the guards are asleep. They have to sleep sometime. Besides, Henry and I both can take care of ourselves with any man."

"If you had to fight, you'd be hopelessly out numbered."

"Girl, you talk like my father," he said with a laugh. "How do you know so much about men's business?"

"I've thought about nothing else for a long time.

I want for you and Victoria and Henry to live happily ever after. Right now, I don't quite see how that's going to happen. If you and Henry go into that hut and make the least sound . . ."

"Like what?"

"Like your sword knocking into something in the dark."

"That would be careless."

"It could happen."

Justin leaned forward, his elbows on his knees, making fists of his hands. "We can fight with knives."

"Against tough men, all armed to the teeth? It scares me."

Justin got up, reached down and pulled her up. "Come on, leave all that to us. Let's find the place and get you back to my mother."

They walked on for a little way, and then, quite suddenly, they heard voices, they saw the flicker of a fire, they heard the stomp of a horse tied up to a tree.

"Stay here," Justin commanded.

He disappeared from her sight, blending himself into the night, not running, but easing from tree to tree until he could get closer to the hut and its guard. He was able to hear a low conversation. He listened carefully as they talked.

"The message is delivered," a low voice said. "The king must come alone. We have him where we want him."

Justin came back to Gina. "This is the place."

He put his hand under her elbow and hurried her back toward the castle. "You may be right. It's better if we don't try to rescue her ourselves. There's a better way. We'll let it seem that the king does come alone. We'll let him agree to give George whatever he wants to free Victoria. Then when he puts her on his horse and rides away, we'll be there, a strong force."

Gina stumbled along beside him. He walked in great strides now, full of energy and eager to plan the rescue.

"Once Victoria and King Richard are back at the castle we can do battle with all of them."

"Do you really think George will keep his word? No matter what the king signs, will he not try to get rid of him and Victoria to serve his own purposes? Wouldn't he simply give orders to kill them both on the spot?"

"Wouldn't that rally every loyal servant of the king against George? Wouldn't that be stirring up a force far bigger than his, to say nothing of Henry's father, who would be outraged?"

Gina stopped on the path, out of breath and frightened. "Oh, Justin, I'm so afraid for Victoria. She could get killed!"

"Please," Justin said, "this is a matter for men to settle. Try to hurry. We must get back to the castle and make our plans."

It seemed to take far longer to get back than it

had to find the hut. Justin left her at the tower where Natalie was waiting for her. She burst into tears as she told Natalie of finding the hut and what Justin's plan was.

"It doesn't make any sense to me," Gina said. "I just can't imagine George letting the king ride off with Victoria, no matter what agreement was signed. Why shouldn't George take everything, not just half."

"That's as may be, Gina," Natalie said, "but women do not plan these things."

"There weren't many guards. They were huddled around a very small fire."

"You may be sure there are enough of them to guarantee the princess is a prisoner who cannot escape."

Gina took off the grey cloak. She was busy thinking. If Victoria could be freed in the dark of the night and reach the castle, then the king would not have to risk his life, and there would be no battle. The combined forces of Henry's father and King Richard would be more than George could hope to combat. He would have to disappear.

There was a knock on the door. When Natalie opened it, there stood Justin and with him another tall, strong looking person.

"Gina, this is Henry. He wants to meet you."

"I wanted to thank you. What you have done will always be remembered, I know, when the story of this land is told. Victoria must be saved, and we will save her. She is essential to the royalty. She is the hope of this nation."

Justin pushed his friend into the room and closed the door.

"He's mad about Victoria," he said with a laugh, "So mad he doesn't think twice about announcing in a loud voice that we will free her."

Henry was as blond as Justin was black haired. His eyes were bright blue and twinkling, not dark like Justin's. For all that he was blond he was not fair skinned but browned by the summer sun.

"We have an audience with the king and my father in half an hour," Henry said. "They are talking together now to make a rescue plan. It's hard to wait. I want to get at it now. All the odds are in our favor. Tomorrow we'll free Victoria." He stepped close to Gina and kissed her hand. "Thank you, Gina, whoever you are. I owe you my life."

"After the meeting, there will be supper in the Great Hall. I'll meet you there," Justin said and they were gone.

Gina remembered the Great Hall full of people as it was the night she had first been there. Now it was half empty, there were only a few torches flaring in their stands, and there was only a small, smoky fire. She and Natalie sat at the end of a table across the room from the raised platform where the king and his guests would eat.

As they took their places, neither the king nor Henry's father wore their crowns. They were not dressed splendidly, they wore belted tunics and swords fastened at their waist, reaching almost to the floor. They were big men, both of them, and with them were Henry and Justin, but not the queen. As soon as they were seated, the servants brought the food. There was cold meat and bread and a plate of apples, very simple fare. When the meal was over, Justin came and sat beside her.

"Henry's father would not agree to letting King Richard go by himself to ransom Victoria. Instead, tomorrow, at dawn, Henry and I are to sneak in while the guards are sleeping, cut Victoria loose and get her outside. She will ride with Henry to the castle. Once we get her out, my father's soldiers will surround the place and take them all prisoner. It should be very easy."

"If you can get into the hut without anyone waking."

"We play games like this all the time. We're pretty good at it. My mother will care for you while I'm gone. By tomorrow noon all our problems will be over, thanks to you!"

He rejoined Henry and the kings, and they withdrew from the hall. Everyone stood up as they left.

There was a gleaming knife that looked like a little sword lying on the fruit plate. Gina pulled the plate close to her and quickly hid the knife in the full sleeve of her blue dress. Her mind was racing. She knew exactly what she was going to do.

When she went to bed in a corner in Natalie's room, she folded the dress carefully, concealing the knife, and laid the grey cloak over it. Everything she needed was in the little pile. Natalie blew out the candles and in just a few minutes she was making little snoring noises. I must wait, Gina thought, for a long time, until everyone here and everyone there is asleep. I must not go to sleep. I must wait.

She lay on her back, looking up into the dark, thinking through every move she must make. If there was an old woman in the hut with Victoria, where would she be? Probably on a bed blocking the doorway. Get by her, get to Victoria, let her know it's me and keep her from making a sound. Cut her loose and get out of the hut silently. Around it to the back, then into the woods.

After that, it should be easy. They would go straight to the king, there would be rejoicing, great thankful joy. The thought of it thrilled her. Then she heard the bells in the bell tower strike the hour of two.

It's much too soon, she told herself, but I just can't lie here. Gina got up silently, put on the blue dress and the cloak, making sure she had the knife as she did. She picked up her shoes in her hand, made her way to the door. It made a sharp squeak. She held her breath, but Natalie did not stir. She slipped out into the dark. She sat on the top step and put on her shoes, holding the knife under her arm.

I have to do this. I have to, so that no one will be hurt. I can slip in and out of that hut much more quietly than Justin or Henry. I'm much smaller. It's what I have to do. She kept saying this to herself as she went down the stairs, across the deserted courtyard, to the little door in the gate Justin had shown her. She knew there were soldiers keeping watch, looking down from the battlements at the top of the castle. There were enough shadows across the bridge to hide her. She moved very carefully, slowly.

The riskiest part was crossing the green to the forest path. She felt the spongy, wet grass under her feet. She crouched low, ran toward the forest path. When she reached it, she leaned against a tree and tried to make her heart stop beating so fast. Soon her eyes adjusted to the dark. She started off again. The rocks in the path seemed much bigger. Without Justin's strong arm pulling her up, it was hard for her to climb over them. Once she tripped and fell, hitting her head on the hard ground. The knife flew out of her hand. She got up very slowly, not sure she could go on. The hut was a long way away.

There were things rustling in the night on both sides of the path. The darkness completely enclosed her. I can't do this, she thought. Fear seemed to take hold of her. Then she heard a calm voice say, "Yes, you can."

A strong feeling of confidence flowed through her. She searched for the knife and found it. Gina started walking again. Even so, she was afraid she might have taken a wrong turn. It seemed so much further than it had with Justin. Her confidence was ebbing when suddenly she recognized the place. There were no voices. No fire. It was deadly still, but she knew she had found the hut.

Tightening her hold on the knife, she took a deep breath and crept closer. Several men were lying on the ground, sprawled in deep sleep. She took only a few steps at a time, stopping to see if anyone stirred, she reached the open door.

Peering inside, she saw a cot just where she thought it would be. An old woman slept with her mouth open, her tangled white hair loose on the straw pillow. Gina felt as if her own breathing was as loud as a windstorm. She breathed more slowly, crept through the door and around the cot, looking for Victoria. She found her lying on a rude cot in a corner.

Her hands were tied behind her, her legs drawn up and tied to the bed post. Just as Gina got to her, she gave a little moan. Gina covered her mouth gently with her hand and whispered, "It's Gina. Hush."

Victoria's eyes flew open in shock, her body jerked.

"Hush," Gina said again. She showed Victoria the knife, then tried cutting the ropes. She couldn't seem to make the knife work. Gina was terrified. What if she couldn't free Victoria? She stopped trying to cut through all the rope at once and attacked separate strands. Then she was able to cut them.

When Victoria stood up, she swayed dizzily. Gina steadied her. They started stepping one foot at a time, inching across the dirt floor like two blind people. Once Victoria lost her balance and fell heavily against Gina. They stood still, holding on to each other until Victoria stepped again. It seemed to take an eternity to get to the door, but they did it. Outside, one of the men turned over and threw an arm up over his head. They stopped again, waiting to see if he was awake. With a little snort he settled down.

Gina kept one hand on the rough wall of the hut and felt their way around to the back. From there they made their way into the protecting woods, walking faster now, until they were out of sight of the hut.

"I have to sit down," Victoria said. "I am so sore from being tied up."

They sat on a rock, still warm from the summer sun. Victoria rubbed her legs and her wrists.

"Gina," she said, "Is this a dream?"

"No," Gina said. "I keep thinking maybe it is, but then, touch me, you'll see, I'm real."

Victoria reached out to her with both hands. "Have you ever been afraid that you were going to die?"

"Not me, but that my sister was going to die. It was awful."

"I prayed. It was a different kind of praying. Somehow I knew that it was the most important prayer of my life. I asked for help, and you came. And now somehow, I know that there is something I must do that no one else can do."

"One day you'll be the queen, and your son will be the king."

Victoria sighed. "I know."

Gina stood up. "We aren't safe yet, come on."

They followed the path to the green. They were almost to the bridge when, out of nowhere, a great figure stepped in front of them with a drawn sword.

"In the name of the king, who are you?" growled a man.

"In the name of which king?" the princess answered haughtily.

"The King of Warwick," came the answer.

"I am his daughter, the Princess Victoria. Take us to him."

With a grunt the man turned. He shouted and other men scrambled to light a torch. He glared at Victoria but one of his men said in a low voice, "That's her. That's the princess. I seen her ride with Justin." The guard led them across the drawbridge and into the dark castle.

"I must find my captain," the man said to Victoria.

"Do that!" Victoria commanded.

It took only a few minutes before Justin's father was summoned, sleepy and confused. He took one look at the bedraggled Victoria and let out a shout of joy.

"What miracle of God is this? Oh, my dear, you are safe!"

Gina was left behind when Justin's father led the princess up the steps to the royal rooms in the highest tower. As they reached the top Victoria looked back.

"Bring Regina Worthington here!" she ordered.

Justin's father looked down at Gina and said, "Who are you?"

"Never mind that now, sir, she is my friend. Take me to my father."

It was, for Gina, as lovely as it would have been had the king been her own father, full of joy to see her safe, having worried himself sick over her. He wept, great tears running down his face, hugging Victoria so tight she struggled to free herself. He had on only a nightshirt, just down to his knees. He didn't look regal at all. He bounded to the bed to wake his wife, shouting, "Annie, Annie! Vicky is safe! She is safe!"

The queen sat up in bed, her hair loosed in a great golden cloud around her head.

"Oh my dearest dear," she cried, "come here to me!"

Victoria rushed to her, and they hugged each other fiercely.

The soldiers withdrew politely, closing the door behind them.

"How in the name of God did this happen?" the king asked, sitting down on the bed beside his wife and child.

"Because of Regina Worthington, Father. I told you, she is my dearest and bravest friend. She freed me all by herself."

The king turned to Gina in the grey cloak. "The maid from the country?" he asked.

"Justin's friend," Victoria said with a secret smile at Gina.

"Justin, is it?" the king scowled. "The plan was . . ."

"Gina has made that plan unnecessary, hasn't she? Neither Justin nor Henry need risk their lives for me."

The king stepped to the door and spoke to Justin's father.

"Please, summon your son and the King of Lancaster's son and bring them to me. My prayers have been answered. There will be no battle tomorrow."

They came, the two young men, with fear on their faces. They thought something terrible had happened, to be summoned to the king in the middle of the night. When they saw Victoria and Regina their delight, their happiness, their gladness was marvelous to see. Henry took Victoria in his arms and Justin swept Gina up and whirled her around. So happy were they that they didn't even ask how it had happened.

"So," the king said, his arm around his wife, "the best, most wonderful happy ending to this miserable affair."

"Victoria," Henry said into her hair, "will you marry me?"

"Yes," Victoria answered. "Yes."

CHAPTER SEVEN
Daring to Imagine

It was still dark outside. Gina and Victoria were together in the princess's room. Neither of them could quiet themselves enough to fall asleep. Natalie had put soothing oil on the bruises left by the ropes on Victoria's wrists and ankles, but every once in a while she would begin shivering.

"Of all my friends, Gina, you are my dearest. You saved me, and you saved all the others from a bloody battle. You must stay with me always. You must be my bridesmaid. You shall be dressed like no other bridesmaid ever. You will be so beautiful."

"You know I cannot stay."

"You must! Don't you know that Justin loves you, too? Why can't you stay?" she demanded.

"My family. I don't want to leave them. My

sister is sick, and she needs me." Gina felt a great stab of guilt. "I want to tell her that the story did come out right, that you will live happily ever after the way she wanted it."

"Sometimes you don't make sense, Gina. What is this story you speak of? Our story, here in Warwick?"

"You and Henry, the king and the queen, Justin and Natalie. I have been telling Beth about you."

"But where is Beth?"

"In York Medical Center, far away."

Gina closed her eyes and a great weariness weighed her down. She felt as if she were being pulled down and down, into darkness deeper than the night. She was so weary that she simply let herself be pulled. Then she heard someone call her name.

When she opened her eyes, it was a bright summer day, the lovely fragrance of wisteria all around her and Mrs. Turner looking at her anxiously.

"When you weren't home, I knew where to find you. Come with me. Beth wants you. They sent me to find you."

"How is she?"

"Stabilized, but restless. We need to get her more peaceful. It's essential. She needs you."

"I can't go to the hospital like this!" Gina protested, looking down at her very short shorts and ragged blouse.

113

"Don't worry about that," Mrs. Turner said with a laugh. "You look exactly like everyone else around here."

They walked together very fast, through the gardens, back up the road, into the medical center. An elevator took them to the top floor. David was standing there, waiting. Without a word he reached out for Gina and hugged her.

"Oh," he said, letting out a great breath, "I'm so glad to see you. I was so worried when we called and you weren't home. Mrs. Turner knew where you were?" Gina nodded and hugged her father close.

"How's Beth?" she asked.

"Not good. There can be only one person with her, they said. She may have taken a turn for the worse. Julia is with her now, but she keeps asking for you."

There was no sunshine in Beth's room. The venetian blinds were closed, the green painted walls made the room seem cool and completely isolated. Beth was lying propped up on pillows, not in a pretty dress or nightie but in a white hospital gown. When Gina and David came in, Julia said, "Here she is, Beth. Here's Gina." Beth opened her eyes and smiled a sad little smile.

"Where were you?" she asked.

"By the wisteria," Gina smiled. "Mrs. Turner knew I'd be there."

David and Julia tiptoed out of the room, David

blowing a kiss at them. Gina sat on the bed. "I have so much to tell you," she said and Beth closed her eyes wearily.

"Good?"

"Very good! I was there, in Warwick again. And it did turn out just as I told you, only it was I who rescued Victoria!"

"You!" Beth exclaimed. She sat up slowly and hugged her knees. "Tell me what happened."

So Gina told how she and Justin had found the hut in the forest bordering the vineyard. She told how the men had made plans for Henry and Justin to rescue Victoria at dawn, and then she said, "I knew that if they did that they could get hurt. If I went while everyone was asleep, I could do it. I knew I could."

"Weren't you scared?"

"Yes, really scared, but I knew I had to do it."

"And now she is going to marry Henry?"

"Yes. And oh, Beth! He is so nice. They will make the finest king and queen anyone has ever imagined."

"What about Justin?" Gina's heart gave a little jump at the sound of his name. She hadn't told Beth of his kiss.

"Well, he will be the second most powerful person in the kingdom when Henry becomes king. He is to be Henry's chancellor. He will have a title and land to go with it. And that's the end of the story, Beth, and it all did turn out just as I said, only better, because I was there, and I know they are all really happy."

"You're sure you weren't just dreaming?"

"I'm sure. I touched people, and they touched me. I heard their voices, saw their faces, and they saw mine. They know me, and I know them."

"But it's a story?"

"Yes, I made it up."

"I keep thinking about it. I wish it weren't over."

The door opened, and a nurse came in. She came to the bed and made Beth lie down.

"Time to rest, now. No more visitors."

Gina kissed Beth's soft cheek, stroked her hair. "Think about them. Think about the beautiful wedding, and maybe next year, a cute baby. Think about Justin, not of royal blood, but living like a prince."

"In a castle with deep, dark water all around it." Beth closed her eyes happily. The nurse made Gina leave.

David and Julia were waiting for her, sitting in straight chairs just outside the door.

The nurse said, "Why don't you all go down to the cafeteria and get some supper? We'll be right here, watching Beth carefully, you may be sure."

So they rode the elevator to the ground floor and found the cafeteria, hearing the clatter of dishes and silver, smelling fried food and onions.

They weren't at all hungry, but they sat at a round table drinking coffee and a Coke.

"What happens now?" Gina asked.

"Dr. Gates will come by this evening, he said. The test results won't be ready until tomorrow morning. They keep on taking them, every hour."

"When he came to the apartment this morning, I couldn't believe how big he is. I hadn't remembered him that way," Gina said.

Julia smiled. "They treat him like a king around here. He sweeps through the halls with about eight people following him all the time."

"I guess he's chief of staff this year," David said. "We're lucky he's Beth's doctor."

"How does she seem to you, Gina?" Julia asked.

"This morning, she wasn't hungry, didn't eat her breakfast. She seemed . . . I don't know . . . far away. Then she was really scared when Dr. Gates came. I was worried about her. But just now, she was almost her old self again."

"She kept asking where you were."

"Do you remember we told you I was making up a story for her, to keep her amused? You said something about Scheher——"

"Scheherezade," David finished. "I remember."

"I feel bad about this, but I think maybe she got upset about the problems my heroine got into."

"You can't make up much of a story without problems for your central character," David said.

"But the whole thing seemed so real to both of us. I even felt it was actually happening to me."

"Gina!" Julia exclaimed.

"It happens," David said. "The mind is an extraordinary thing. It can create a world, just thinking. Think of the science fiction worlds some great writers have created. They are vivid, with details that are thrilling."

"Last Sunday the dean said in his sermon that he knew that the people listening to him came from different worlds, like the world of science, and medicine, or the world of art."

"Did you tell your father about that sermon?" Julia asked.

"He talked about you, David. He said lots of nice things about you and the book. You're going to preach next week?"

David whistled. "I completely forgot that." He looked very seriously into his empty coffee cup. Gina thought he was thinking about a sermon topic, but he was not. He said, "What is reality, you asked me, before all this with Beth. You were deep into the story then?" She loved it when he talked to her so intently. She always felt closest to him when they discussed things on that level.

"First, I made up the story out of words, ideas. I tried to make it sound like stories Julia used to read to me. I looked at pictures of castles and queens and handsome heroes. I thought about it a lot, the story. I made up scenes from the pictures. Then I . . . you won't believe this . . . I somehow was actually there, in the castle, talking to the people in the story, and they were talking to me. And I got involved in the story myself."

"What are you saying?" Julia was incredulous.

"Wait, Julia," David said quietly. "This is Gina's wonderfully creative mind. She used it to amuse Beth. You asked me what is real, Gina? I've asked myself the same thing. There's no simple answer. In New York one of the questions Peter Ames asked me was how did I know I hadn't made up this world of the Spirit I'm so devoted to. How did I know it wasn't a kind of daydreaming." He fell silent, the noise of the surrounding room invaded their space.

Julia shook her head. "Listen, you two, this is getting too deep. Let's go back upstairs. I want to know that Beth is all right."

"Sure," David said, getting up slowly and gathering the coffee cups and Gina's Coke glass. "But Gina, I know when I center my mind in the world of the Spirit, it is as real as this cafeteria."

In the elevator they shot up to the top floor and her father, standing next to Gina, lost his balance for a moment as they came to a jolting stop. He fell against her shoulder. To right himself he put his arm around her and said very softly, "We're two of a kind, kiddo, aren't we?"

Beth was fast asleep when they came to her room. There was nothing to do but sit in the hall and wait for Dr. Gates.

There were only two men following him as he arrived. They went into Beth's room without knocking, just walked right in. Gina listened to the clock on the wall jump every few minutes for what seemed a very long time. David got up and walked down to the charge desk and back. Still, they waited. At last the door opened and Dr. Gates and the other two came out.

"It's quite unusual," Dr. Gates said to David. "This morning there was a clear possibility of a relapse. It has disappeared! We'll wait for the test results, but I have a good feeling that Beth is back on track."

"Thanks be to God!" David said fervently.

"Indeed!" Dr. Gates put his hand on David's arm, and Gina saw the nice Dr. Gates who had comforted her mother. "I want to know more about your God, David. I'm looking forward to next Sunday when you preach."

The lights blinked in the hall. A voice said visitors must leave. They each said goodnight to Beth, assured her that they'd be back in the morning. They left her with a sweet-faced nurse.

When they got home, Gina suddenly thought about Eliot's call.

"He wants you to call him when you can," she told David.

David looked at his watch. "I guess it's not too late." He went into his study. Gina started up the stairs to her room.

"Are you feeling okay?" her mother asked her.

Gina turned, looking down at her mother, "I'm

much better now that Beth is better."

"It's been a bad day for me," Julia said, coming up to where Gina was standing. "I worry about all of you. I worry about Beth. I worry about your father and how his whole life has changed so much in such a short time. And I worry about you doing all this fantasizing. I know people do it when they are lonely, or when they feel depressed." Gina and Julia walked together to the top of the stairs.

"I'm not lonely or depressed."

"Without actually realizing how much we were asking of you, we just gave you so much responsibility. We took away your own life from you." They stopped at the door to Gina's bedroom.

"You and David and Beth are my life."

"But your friends . . ."

Gina stood very still for a moment, thinking about them. They seemed ten thousand miles away, very small, like looking through the wrong end of a telescope.

"You and David have let me be part of everything you do, every decision you make. We've shared the happy times and the hard times. I have always felt so lucky about it. I don't know anyone else whose mother and father do that."

"We've managed a pretty good way of living that works for us, haven't we? Only now I wonder if maybe we are going to have to change everything."

Gina went into her room and sat down on the bed. Julia came and sat beside her.

"You mean Eliot and everything?"

"Yes. Not just Eliot either. Imagine being invited to preach at York Chapel, an associate professor in a very small state college? It's amazing. Imagine being interviewed on national television, being reported on the evening news? We've never had much money and now we actually are going to have to figure out what to do with a bigger income."

"Julia?" David called.

"With Gina," she called back.

They heard him come up the steps, two at a time.

"Eliot is going crazy. The book won a book-of-the-year award from the American Theological Association, and he tells me I must accept the honor in Boston next month. His boss is making his life miserable because the publishers want a commitment from me, right now. He insists I write a sequel, and that I co-operate with the sales promotions, although they are terrific at the moment. He wants to come to talk to me, but I told him no. What with Beth and preparing that sermon and teaching my classes I have no time for him this week. He's miffed at me. I don't blame him, but that's the way it is."

David loosened his tie, sat on a chair next to the bed, looking unhappy.

"I can't commit to anything until we know from the doctors what the picture is for Beth. I still have a big commitment to my students here this summer. I need to concentrate on my teaching, finish up the course properly. I don't care about book promotion or interviews. I begin to be very uncomfortable with this whole thing. I'm losing control of my life."

Julia stood up and went to him. "Come to bed, David. You must be exhausted. All of us need to get some sleep."

He got up and rubbed his eyes. "You're right. Good night, Gina." He leaned over and kissed her. "Love you," he said.

In the morning they went through their usual breakfast routine, except they didn't fix a tray for Beth. David called the hospital and was told that Beth had slept well, had already eaten a fair breakfast. The tests were ready for Dr. Gates.

"I have my eight o'clock class, then I'll get over to the hospital. I'll call you both from there."

"I'll tell Dr. Glover I may have to leave again today. He's been very nice about it but he's expecting me in class this morning," Julia said, fastening a bright earring on her ear.

"You go on, both of you," Gina said, "I'll wash up here."

David drank the last of his coffee. "After Sunday we have only two weeks more at York." He seemed to be talking as much to himself as to Gina and Julia. "Teaching here is clearly an honor I appreciate. I'm aware of the prestige of the place every minute, every hour. Really to belong here . . . well, it's pretty august company."

"The dean said he hoped you would stay," Gina declared.

"I expect the invitation to preach will have something to do with any such idea. That puts far too much importance on a simple sermon." He checked his watch, got up quickly. "I'm off," he said, gathering books and briefcase from the table in the hall. "Be good, both of you. I'll call shortly after nine."

Gina washed all the dishes and put them away. She went upstairs and made her bed, looked in to see that her parents' bed was made. One of the best ways to kill time, she told herself, is to do something you really don't want to do. So she cleaned both the upstairs bathrooms thoroughly. She spent quite a little time polishing the glass shower doors, pleased when they sparkled and shone. Finally, the phone rang. She rushed downstairs.

It wasn't David, however, it was Eliot.

"How's Beth?" he asked. Gina told him they would soon know.

"It's not a crisis any more?"

"No, she seems better."

"Then I'm coming. I'll get the first plane out of here and be there sometime this afternoon. Does David have many classes?"

"He has one at two o'clock and an hour of conferences."

"Tell him I'll be there at four. I'll only take an hour of his time, but it's crucial, got that? It's crucial."

Gina started to say that her father was awfully busy, had said he didn't have time for Eliot, but somehow it seemed wrong. She told him she'd be sure to tell David, and she hung up. She looked at the clock in the kitchen. It was not yet nine o'clock. I need to find a book to read, she thought, something to occupy my mind. She went to her father's studio where he kept a lot of books. She started looking at them, got closer and closer to his desk. An open book was lying there and she could see that he had underlined, in red pencil, a sentence halfway down the page. It said, "Why not dare to imagine a career as a 'great' preacher?" He had crossed out "preacher" and in his careful handwriting had written "writer".

Why not dare to imagine . . . what a wonderful idea.

And then the phone did ring. It was David and he said things couldn't be better. They were bringing Beth home. The joy in his voice filled Gina's heart with happiness. She forgot all about Eliot.

They brought Beth home, her father and the same two men in the ambulance, and they carried her back up the stairs in a grand procession, making Beth giggle at their antics.

Gina fixed lunch, and they ate together in Beth's room. While she was eating, enjoying the release of fear about Beth, she looked at her father and thought, "there is no limit to what a person can dare to imagine. He is already more than halfway there."

Then she remembered Eliot. "I forgot to tell you," she said, and David turned to her with concern. "Eliot is coming."

"Coming here?" David exploded.

"This afternoon at four. I told him your schedule."

"I told him not to come. He's the most stubborn man I ever knew. Did he say what he wants?"

"Only that it will take about an hour."

"I know what it is. He wants me to let the publishers run my life. He wants me to say I'll tour the country like a traveling salesman."

"No!" Beth said in a loud voice. "You can't. We need you."

David went to the bed quickly. "None of you needs me as much as I need you, honey," he said, stroking her long hair. His manner was so tender that she calmed down at once.

"But right now the university runs my life, so I must go. Be nice to Eliot if I'm a little late from my conference. I have a student who loves to talk. Beth, remember what they told you. You still need to rest as much as you can to keep on doing so well."

Gina read to Beth out of Mrs. Turner's book about gardens until she went to sleep. Then, tiptoeing downstairs, she did the dishes she had left in the sink. She decided to make brownies to offer to Eliot, and found all the ingredients she would need. There was a lovely smell of chocolate and brewing coffee when he arrived and she could see that he was pleased to be welcomed.

At Hansford, Eliot and her father had worked for endless hours together. Eliot had always seemed charged up, always seemed full of energy. Today he seemed tired.

"These are wonderful, Gina," he said, helping himself to a third brownie.

"David said to be nice to you in case he's late. He said he has a conference with a student who likes to talk."

"It's just like David, isn't it, not to say 'time's up'? I've never known anyone who loves the kids he teaches as much as he does." Eliot stirred his coffee thoughtfully. "I guess he'd miss teaching, even for a year. But Hansford is such a backwoods place; he's outgrown it."

"What do you mean?" Gina was stung by the remark.

"He'd be better off, if he must teach, at a place like this one. York. It's first class. It's a great university."

"Hansford is a great college, I think," Gina said, "and besides it's home."

"Don't you want your father to succeed? He has everything going for him, right now. He's just got to step up and seize the opportunities that have opened up."

"He's got to dare to dream?"

"You bet. And he can do it."

"Do what?" David laughed as he came in, shook hands with Eliot, and seemed very glad to see him. Gina wasn't sure about that.

"Let's talk about it," Eliot said earnestly.

"What smells so good?" David asked Gina, dumping all his books, a pile of papers and his briefcase on a chair.

"You've got her nicely trained, David. She made me brownies, my very favorite food." He ate a fourth.

"We never had to train Gina to be sweet. She's always been that way from the day she was born, which I remember as if it were today. Now tell me what brings you all this way in such a hurry, even when I asked you not to come?"

Gina was aware that these two men really liked each other, but that there was a lot of tension between them.

"First, this." Eliot put a check in front of David.

"Goodness!" he said. "Takes my breath away!"

Eliot looked at him fondly.

David said, "Julia and I have worked all summer for less than half of this."

"I'm told there will be more, David. I had to

come to make you see what a tremendous opportunity these people are offering you."

"These people?" David poured himself a cup of coffee before he sat down. "That's just it, Eliot, I don't want to let these people take over. They want to change my life completely."

Eliot pounded his fist into his hand, "But you want to sell your ideas, don't you? You want people to explore the world of the spirit and catch that thrill of adventure you're so keen on. New York proved to all of us that you are terrifically effective speaking in person. You can reach ordinary people, maybe more than would read the book."

David reached for a brownie, ate it in two bites. "New York proved to me that I hate leaving my family, hate hotel rooms, hate working with people who not only don't know what I'm talking about, but don't care, either."

"Nothing is accomplished without some sacrifice."

"Ah," David pushed his chair back from the table. "You're going to push that button? Right now, at least, I don't believe sacrifice is needed. I do think I am called. I think I am even empowered to bring a simple message about developing a spiritual life, and . . ."

"You are," Eliot interrupted. "Now take it out to where the people are. Both Hansford and York are too confining for you."

David shook his head, his face intent, his mouth

a straight line. "No. At Hansford I live with people who love what they do. They constantly explore new ideas. They get excited about learning about the universe. History, for them, is a fascinating, unfolding drama. They spend hours drawing and painting. They practice all day long to have the technique to make beautiful music."

He stood up and walked to the sink, leaning against it. Then he turned and looked at Eliot. "I get to know students, a new crop every year. Their minds are sharp. Their outlook different from mine. There is nothing confining about Hansford College."

Eliot was exasperated. He threw up both hands in the air. "So what's the bottom line?" David walked back across the room.

"As soon as we can, we're going back to Hansford. No deal."

Eliot stared at David. He sighed a great sigh. He shoved both hands deep into his pockets. He shook his head, looked defeated. "You will write another book? At least give me that."

"Maybe more than one."

"I guess I have to settle for that. I hope I can keep my job."

David smiled. "I don't think you have a problem. But come and see our wonder child. It seems she has almost healed herself."

The room was full of sunshine, but Beth was

still fast asleep. When David stood by her bed, she stirred sleepily.

"Wake up, Sleeping Beauty," he said, "Your friend Eliot is here."

She opened her eyes, saw her father, and reached out her arms. He leaned over and hugged her. She happily snuggled against him when he sat down and held her. From within the circle of his arm she said, "Hello, Eliot."

"Hello, wonder child," he said, coming close. "It's good to see you well again."

"Am I well enough to see the gardens?" Beth asked.

"Soon," David answered, "soon."

That whole week David spent every evening in his study. Gina went to bed long before he climbed the steps and turned out the lights. She heard him walking softly down the hall. Then she would turn over and go to sleep.

On Sunday morning he made French toast with an apron tied over his best black Sunday pants. It was a real celebration because they brought Beth downstairs for the first time. David did everything with a flourish. They laughed at his jolly manners. Gina couldn't believe how happy she felt.

"One more week of classes," David said. "Then exams, and grading papers. Then home to Hansford. But today is my big day."

They had just finished the last bite when Mrs. Turner arrived.

"Just look at our Beth," David said, untying the apron. "Thanks to you and all the good people at the medical center she's almost as good as new."

Mrs. Turner hugged Beth and reached out a hand to Gina.

"Your Gina, Mr. Worthington, has all the qualities of a fine nurse."

Except, Gina thought, that she upset her patient with her wild storytelling. David put on his black suit coat.

"I must get myself over to the chapel. Please pray for me."

When Gina and Julia got to the chapel it was already full. There was not an empty seat to be seen. The choir was standing just outside the wide red doors, and the clergy were gathering, too. One of the solemn looking ushers approached and said, "Mrs. Worthington, there are seats reserved for you up front. May I escort you?" He offered Julia his arm, and another younger man stepped up to Gina, and she took his arm. The four of them walked down the main aisle of the splendid chapel. The organ was weaving a prelude around the opening hymn. Gina knew that people were staring at them. It reminded her of seating the mother of the bride at a wedding, except that Julia looked younger than a bride's mother would be. Just as they reached their seats the organ burst forth with "There's a Wideness in God's Mercy," one of Gina's favorite hymns. She wondered if her father had chosen it, and as the service went on, she was sure he had.

She had to tip her head back to see him when he climbed the steps into the pulpit. She had seen him often before in flowing academic robe, the scarlet hood on his back. To Gina, no one in all the world looked so distinguished. He took a moment to look out at the overflowing congregation. People were now standing up and down both side aisles. He said in a clear and vibrant voice, "Grace to you, and peace, from God the Father, God the Son and God the Holy Spirit, Alleluia, Amen."

"Alleluia, Amen," the crowd responded enthusiastically and took their seats.

She had heard him do it many, many times, but she marveled at the way he always seemed to make people listen to every word. He seemed full of joy. The way he looked, the way he spoke from his heart, the way he used his sensitive hands, it was the way he always did at home in Hansford. But here, in this magnificent place, it was totally impressive. She sat there, not really listening, just loving him.

She knew her mother was loving him, too, but that she was deeply concentrating on what he was saying. So Gina listened.

"Imagination is the process of forming mental

images of things remembered or something that is not or had not before been seen or experienced. With creativity we imagine scenes and people and sometimes they seem as real as this scene right here. All week I have been imagining it, and here it is, just as I saw it. The power of human imagination is infinite. It was created by God. It is a gift to be used, to be cultivated, to enhance our lives."

Her mother touched Gina's hand and smiled at her. Gina remembered David saying "We are two of a kind." She knew he meant their vivid imaginations.

But Warwick . . . was Warwick something she created that wasn't there before she imagined it? Why did she resist that idea? Because Justin had said "You didn't make us up; you found us somehow." Gina closed her eyes. She had been forcing herself not to think about Justin, not to think about Victoria and the king and queen.

They don't exist, she told herself. Something said to her "But they do." In an instant her whole heart and mind were filled with the memory of Justin's kiss. She had forbidden herself to think about it so many times. But now the joy of it swept through her.

The people all around her said a loud Amen. It was time to recite the Nicene Creed. She stood, and the memory dissolved into the real world around her.

It took Gina and Julia more than ten minutes

to reach the doors of the chapel. People seemed in no hurry to leave, talking in little groups and making their way slowly down the aisles to where the clergy greeted them. David was surrounded with men and women, all expressing their admiration. The dean stood by him, taking in all their comments like a beaming father.

A tall, elderly, white-haired man who looked very important, shook hands with the dean and then held out his hand to David. "Not since Travis Ruskin preached here twenty years ago have I heard a sermon like that. It was pure genius."

"Thank you, sir," David said.

"It's who you are as well as what you say, young man. There's a glow about you, and we both know where that comes from."

He moved along and others followed until only Julia and Gina were left.

"My wife and my daughter," David said to the dean.

"Gina!" the dean's eyes lit up.

"And Julia," David added, putting his arm around his wife.

"Do an old man a favor, you nice young people," the dean said affably. "Come to my office before you take your deserved sabbath rest. There is something very important I want to talk about."

The dean had no gold crown, but to Gina, as he sat behind the huge mahogany desk in the plush dean of the chapel's office, he might as well have been a king. Her mother and father and she sat in a small ring of chairs facing him. He folded his hands under his chin and seemed to be in deep thought for a moment.

"We have no vacancies on the theological faculty here at York," he said, "but we want to keep you here, David. Your ability to attract young people is outstanding. Your counseling at the hospital has been enormously effective and helpful. You are a gifted preacher."

He stopped, put both hands flat on his desk and leaned forward.

"I've been trying to find a way for us to offer you enough of a challenge that you might take some risks with us. I have a very preliminary plan. For a long time I've had this idea of developing a bold new curriculum in theology for our continuing education program. Admission would be open to everyone, no requirements. I firmly believe in the priesthood of all believers. Actually, people who take these courses now are graduate level people looking for refreshment."

The three of them waited for him to go on. Gina could see that David was looking puzzled.

"Perhaps you would consider appointment to the continuing education faculty? Unfortunately, they can offer one year contracts only. But you would have the entire resources of York University at your command. There was a general feeling of enthusiasm when I mentioned this idea to a high level board meeting. There are wonderful minds eager to work on the project."

"The idea is to design a whole new course of study?"

"Yes. Designed to make church members informed ministers."

"And when it is designed . . . ?"

"If it captures the imagination of enough people, then you'd be in charge of making it work. I had in mind a title for the program: Faith Seeking Understanding."

"Sir," David began, but the dean interrupted him.

"This must be a family decision, I know. There is much to be considered. Come and talk to me after you've thought about it."

He stood up. Gina had the feeling he wanted terribly to know what David was thinking.

"It would be a totally new adventure for me," David said quietly. "A whole new direction. First the book, now this!"

"That's what I like about you. You turn everything into an adventure."

They left the dean's office and walked home silently.

"What can I say?" David said as they opened the door to the apartment. "I keep thinking that all of us belong at Hansford College. Gina and Beth with their friends in school, Julia going on with her research and I . . . I long for my quiet, uneventful life there."

"I'm amazed at you," Julia said. "He's offered you the chance of a lifetime, I would say."

"You're willing to take a chance? It might not work. I haven't had any experience in designing programs like this."

"Faith seeking understanding, he said. That's what you're all about, David."

"I need to support my family for a long time, Julia. The one year part scares me."

The three of them went upstairs to Beth's room. She was sitting at a card table playing double solitaire with Mrs. Turner.

"Finish this game for me, will you, Gina?" Mrs. Turner said. "I'm to meet my son, Kevin, at the airport in exactly one hour. It will be wonderful to have him home again. He wants to meet all of you. He loved the book as much as I thought he would." She smiled at David.

So Gina finished the game and David and Julia went down to the kitchen. Gina could hear them talking as they started lunch together.

"Was David good?" Beth asked.

"Very good. The dean wants him to stay here."

"I don't want to stay here."

"You haven't had a chance to see how beautiful it is."

138

Beth pouted. "I don't care about that. I just want to go home, don't you?"

"I guess I'd rather go home, sure, but there's something about living here that's special."

"Makes you think of kings and queens and stories?"

"It's more than that . . . I don't know."

"I'm convinced," David said at lunch, "that God has a plan for each of us. The trick is to separate our plans from God's plan."

"What do you think it would be like, working on the dean's project?" Gina asked. "What would you be doing?"

"Good question, Gina," David said. "Really to know what you're talking about when you say you are a Christian means studying and learning and spiritual discipline. History and tradition, the great religions, mysticism and spirituality, that's what we'd be working with. I've always found that the more I learn about these things the more exciting it gets."

Gina saw Julia smile at David. "Imagine it, David, working with scholars here, fashioning something new, never done before, getting lots of people involved in it, bringing together their knowledge."

"Like your work in Gothic architecture and philosophy . . . how the cathedrals shaped the people's lives . . . ?"

"It seems to me there are infinite possibilities."

"Woman, you are leading me on!" David laughed happily.

"Not I, I think. We are being led."

The next day was a big one for Beth. She stood on her feet for the very first time since the illness struck. With Joanie, her physical therapist, holding her one side and Gina on the other, they gradually let her go. It lasted only for a few seconds but Joanie and Gina burst into cheers, laughed and danced and cried for joy.

"It still may take many months until you're really well, but this is a major step forward," Joanie said before she left.

David came home for lunch, and he too joined their happiness. He had a glow of happiness himself. He had spent the whole morning with the dean.

"There's a new private school for faculty kids," he told Gina, "and the dean thinks both you and Beth will love it. What do you think about all this, Gina?"

"Julia thinks it's what we should do. Until now, I haven't thought of how anything might be until Beth is well again. Taking care of her is still my whole life. But maybe . . . "

"Maybe there's a new life for you here," David finished. "Maybe for all of us."

When Julia came home just before supper time she said, "I walked through the gardens on the way home, Gina. You have to see the chrysanthemums. Every color you ever could imagine, just absolutely beautiful! Put on a sweater and go see them!"

The sun was low in the sky making everything look as if it were lit like a stage. She walked through the deserted campus, past the chapel, down the path to the gardens.

Sure enough, the chrysanthemums were spectacular. All alone she felt surrounded with beauty, uplifted by it.

As she came to the center of the garden, she couldn't believe her eyes. Justin was standing there! She ran to him.

"Justin!" she cried joyfully.

He looked startled, surprised. Then he smiled, a warm, friendly smile. "No, I'm Kevin Turner."

Gina gasped, overcome.

Kevin said, "Are you Gina Worthington by any chance?"

Gina nodded.

"My mother loves your whole family. I think your father is wonderful. His book has changed my life."

He looked at her with great curiosity, seeing that she was somehow stunned or confused. "What?" he said.

"I thought you were somebody else," she managed to say.

"It's strange." He reached out and took her hand. "You look familiar to me, too. Have we met somewhere?"

"I think so," Gina whispered, feeling the warmth of his hand.

"It must have been in this garden . . . but surely, I would remember . . ."

How can this be happening? Gina thought. Everything about him is exactly like Justin.

"Anyway, I can see you're a lot like your father. Mom says he's going to be here at York this year. Ever since I was in grammar school I've wanted to go to college here. I just got accepted!"

He pulled her arm through his just the way Justin did. He smiled at her just the way Justin smiled. "I'm so glad I found you, Gina Worthington. This is going to be a wonderful year."

He looked down at her, his dark eyes dancing. He didn't kiss her, but he looked as if he wanted to, just for a minute.